Black Dawn

Misty Kemp

I want to dedicate this book to my best friends. My sisters, who are always with me through thick and thin. Not matter the situation life brings.

Contents

CHAPTER ONE

Cadence

MAY 12, 2006

I ABSOLUTELY DETEST THE feeling of being rushed, especially when I'm late for something important. And it's my own fault. I forgot to set the alarm. Even knowing how big today is, I still forgot.

So now, I'm doing what I hate most: rushing through a shower and getting ready for my very last day at Cape High School.

It is a bittersweet moment in my life. It really is. I am thrilled for this chapter of my life to be coming to an end, but a lot has happened just over the last four years. My high school years were not wasted, though. Needless to say, I tried to make the most of them.

I'm proud of my accomplishments, every single one hard-earned. I worked tirelessly to maintain straight A's and, with that, earned valedictorian. Other things, like being crowned prom and homecoming queen, were unexpected but came with being one of the most popular students in school.

Still, I'll be a little sad. I'll have to say goodbye to most of my friends. Some are off to college, some to the military, and others are just moving away.

One friend, though, the most important one, will be sticking by my side like glue. There's no separating us.

"Cadence!" My mother's voice carries up from downstairs.

I gather up my purse and keys before making my way down to join my mother in the kitchen. I know she will not let me leave the house without eating something.

"Good morning, Mom." I greet her with a smile. I set my bag down on the edge of the bar, then take the stool that I normally use every morning.

I look up at my mother as she sets the plate down in front of me. From the outside looking in, my mother and I could almost pass as twins. At the very least, as sisters, given the twenty-year difference between us.

And I'm not being conceited when I say that my mother, Carol Robinson, is beautiful. Her straight black hair grazes her shoulders, her slender frame is graceful, and her fawn-colored skin is flawless.

The only difference is our eyes, hers a bright blue, mine a deep jade green. My hair is much longer, trimmed only twice a year, and so dark it sometimes shimmers blue or purple in the light.

My mother turns back toward me again, setting a glass of milk in front of me, pulling me from my thoughts. She has a bright smile on her face.

Tomorrow is not only my eighteenth birthday, but I also graduate from high school. Another bittersweet moment.

I lean into the plate in front of me to inhale the heavenly aroma coming from the plate. Bacon, eggs, and buttered toast, with grape jelly on the side. One of my favorite breakfasts. "Fantastic now, but I am running late." I start on the eggs. They are fried to perfection, just like always.

Mom sits beside me. "I understand you're running late, but we need to talk about something quickly."

I nod, still eating.

"Your grandparents..." She pauses. I know she means my father's parents; hers died in a car accident sixteen years ago, when I was too young to remember them. "...will be here tonight, or at the latest, tomorrow morning, for your graduation ceremony."

As soon as the words left her mouth, I gasped, aspirating the bite of egg that I had just placed into my mouth. I guess my ability to eat and listen at the same time malfunctioned. The bite of egg felt like it was firmly lodged in the back of my throat and refused to move in either direction. I instantly start to cough, attempting to clear the foreign object from my windpipe. "What?!"

She just chuckled at my reaction, but she at least started to pat me on my back. Her being a nurse, she knew that if I was talking and coughing, I could breathe. "I understand that this is unusual. However, this is an important year for you. Not only are you turning eighteen, but you also graduate from high school. You know there are no repeats in life. If they want to see these important events, they must be here."

I set the glass down gently, much gentler than I am feeling. My throat seemed to be working properly once again. "That has never concerned them in the past," I state with a sneer.

Traditionally, I see my grandparents once a year. For my entire life, it has been this way. On New Year's Eve, my only living grandparents would make the drive from some small town in Texas to where we live in Missouri. They would arrive around noon. And would be gone twenty-four hours later. It never changes.

I'm not even sure where in Texas they live. I've never been there. Cards, money, and phone calls fill the rest of the year, but seeing them in person is different.

"Why would this birthday be any different from the last seventeen?" I mutter.

She shakes her head like she doesn't know the answer either. "You know they love you." She pauses to wait for a response that is not coming. "It's just with their jobs, whatever it is that they do, are so demanding they get almost no free time to disappear for a few days at a time. Maybe if we lived closer, we would see them more often," she finishes when I don't answer. "Maybe if we lived closer, we'd see them more."

I've heard this explanation for years. I do know they love me, but one day a year never felt like enough. I wanted the kind of closeness my friends had with their grandparents. Eventually, I stopped asking.

What kind of job makes you work all but three days a year? No vacations, no sick leave; it's absurd. If it's legitimate, it's one job I'd never want.

"This year is important..." Mom starts again, probably sensing my thoughts running away from me. "They didn't say more, just that they'll be here for your birthday and graduation."

Just as I start to respond, I catch a glimpse of the clock on the wall behind her head. "Oh, crap!" I jump up, grabbing my purse and the last slice of bacon off my plate. I will have to eat it on the run. "I got to go, Mom; I am going to be late." I lean down to kiss her on the cheek before rushing to the door.

Before the door closed behind me, I called back to my mom. "Love you. See you later." I could not or would not leave without saying the words that were drilled into me. Since the day my maternal grandparents died. You never know if you will get another chance.

By the time I made it to the student parking lot outside Cape High, I could hear the bell ringing. I am officially late. I speed-walked down the halls. The last thing I need is to be stopped; that would just make me even later.

I slip into the back of Mr. Smith's, our homeroom teacher, class well after the bell has run. I am surprised I did not catch him mid-sentence. He is still sitting behind his desk. He just smiles at me, taps his watch a couple of times, and shakes his head. At this point, what can they really do? This is the last day of school. Half of the class is not even here at all.

"Good morning," my best friend greets with a snicker.

I take my seat and glance at her. Madison Miller is my opposite, the yin to my yang. Her golden hair sparkles in the sunlight streaming through the windows, and her hazel eyes are the perfect blend of green and brown.

She's slightly shorter than my five-foot-ten frame, giving her a fuller appearance, with more curves than me.

We've been inseparable since the day her family moved onto my street. I was riding my new bike, training wheels and all, when she came outside and asked if we could ride together.

"Why are you so late?" she whispers.

"I'll tell you later," I mouth back, turning my attention to Mr. Smith as he stands and leans against the front of his desk, just like every other day this year.

"Welcome to your last day of high school." He pauses to let everyone cheer.

Once everyone is calmed down once again, he smiles. "Today is going to be a little bit different than you expected. Today is all about memories and fun." He looks around the class.

"There's a blank piece of paper on everyone's desk." He pauses again as students fidget with their papers. "Well… I hope it's still blank," he says, looking directly at the football captain, Ethan Ellis. "If it's not, please take another from an empty desk." Ethan and two others quickly grab replacements.

"These papers will be used to compose a letter to a random first-year student. The letters will be given to freshmen on their first day this fall. This tradition has been part of this school for over thirty years." His expression softens with nostalgia. "I still have my own freshman letter, and I'm sure a few of you do as well. Now, please take the next few minutes to write yours. When you're done, fold it into thirds." He stands and returns to his desk.

Madi smiles, then turns to the paper in front of her. I do the same. We had just talked about these letters yesterday, so we already knew exactly what we were going to write. Time to put pencil to paper.

Five minutes later, I set my pencil down and glance over to find my friend staring at me with that look, the one that says she's waiting for me to explain why I was late. She knows how I feel about the subject. I swivel my chair to face her completely.

"So, get this... my grandparents are coming to town. They'll be here sometime tonight or first thing in the morning."

Madi's mouth drops open. "Really?"

I nod. "Honestly, I'm astonished." I recount the conversation I had with my mother that morning, then shrug, making it clear I'm just as clueless. "I have no idea why this year, or this event, would be any

different from my past achievements."

Before she can respond, Mr. Smith speaks again. "All right, it looks like everyone's finished. Please pass your letters to the front of your row."

Students begin following his instructions. Once the letters are stacked at the front, he walks by to collect them. "Now, one at a time, starting with Mr. Ellis, please come up here, pick a shirt in your size, and return to your seat."

I wait patiently until it is my turn, and then I stand to go pick out my own shirt. What I find when I reach the front is a T-shirt that has the school's name and the "Class of 2006" written on the front in a pretty font. It also has our mascot. I take the shirt in my size and return to my seat.

When the last student sits down, Mr. Smith addresses us again. "These shirts are a gift from all your teachers," he says warmly. "This way, you'll have another memory from your time here at Cape High. You may now move around the room for the next few minutes to give everyone a chance to sign each other's shirts."

Before he can even finish speaking, I snatch Madi's shirt right off her desk, signing it in a large spot right in the center of the backside, making sure that my area, as her best friend, takes up the most space. She grabs my shirt and does the same. For the next half an hour, everyone is doing the same, some moving to other people and others waiting. When the last of us is finished and everyone is seated again, Mr. Smith stands up.

"All right, everyone, calm down for just a second." He waits until everyone is quiet. "Please leave all of your belongings here and quietly make your way to the gymnasium for the awards assembly," he pauses. "Please return here once the assembly is over."

We all stand at once but wait until it is our row's turn to leave. We all know the drill, since they have taught us to leave in this manner since we were in the first grade.

CHAPTER TWO

Cadence

Since only the seniors received awards this morning, the entire assembly only took about two hours. I walked away with several honors, which was expected, considering everything I've accomplished over the years. All of my awards would be officially presented at graduation tomorrow.

Madi and I make our way back to the class and find that all our belongings are missing. The shirts we all had just signed, our bags, and anything else we had on our desks are just gone. In their place is a single note card.

"What the heck?" Madi exclaims. We rush to our desks and each pick up the card. I read mine aloud:

"I was here, but now I am gone. To get me back, you must work as a team, but only in pairs. Follow the clues to get to the end. Good luck on your journey, and take care, all of you."

I glance up at Madi, then turn to look around the room. A few of the note cards are already gone. "What does this mean..." She pauses, and both of our faces light up with excitement.

"A scavenger hunt," we say together, grinning.

I hadn't been in one since I was a little girl, the last time when we were about ten. I wasn't sure why they weren't done more often, or why I'd never been signed up for any. Maybe that's why I loved them so much.

Unable to hold back our excitement, we flip the card over and read the first clue aloud:

"The first place to go is the first place you went the first time you were here on your first day of school."

At the bottom was a hint:

"I also greet every guest but never say a word."

A look of confusion crosses Madi's face. "Where did we go first? Would it be the office or homeroom?"

I am already shaking my head. "No, that can't be right. We didn't go to the office at all on our first day. Everything was handled ahead of time at registration."

I think back to that day. We'd already had our schedules. Since we were returning students, everything was finalized at the end of the previous year on registration day, when we just confirmed our information and signed the necessary forms.

A few more students walk in as we speculate. "What happened to our stuff?" a blonde girl asks. I stay quiet, competitiveness kicking in, and keep my focus on the clue.

"Look here," another student says; I am not sure who. I do not even look up to see.

About that time, Madi grabs my arm and starts to pull me from the classroom. If this is a contest of any kind, we do not want to give the others our answers. "I got it. If this is a contest, we're not giving anyone our answers," she whispers.

She starts to pull me down the hall but does not say anything until we are out of earshot of the other students. "I know where to go." She does not say any more about it, but I know where she is going. I have figured it out as well.

The front entrance had been the first place we went on our first day. All students were funneled through it because all other doors were locked. Staff marked us off as we entered.

It does not take long to reach the front doors. All along the outside frame, there are multiple white envelopes taped up around the frame. I hurry over to it, pull one envelope off, and open it to reveal the second clue.

"I am always there to give comfort and care, even when you are being a bear."

We don't need to discuss it. The answer is obvious: the school nurse. Unfortunately, the nurse's office is in the elementary building across the street; our school isn't big enough for its own.

We dart across the crosswalk, slowing only when a car approaches. Safety first. Getting hit by a speeder wouldn't help us win. We get our fair share of fast drivers here.

When we reach the elementary doors near the nurse's office, we don't slow down. The nurse just laughs as we burst in, then hands an envelope to Madi, who is closest.

Madi opens it and reads aloud:

"To find the next clue, you will have to think; You'll use one of these if you need a drink."

"What?" I ask. "I mean, I know the answer and then again… I don't." Madi looks from the card to me with a curious expression on her face.

"How many water fountains are there in the high school?" she asks, but I do not know the answer either. We could really be searching all day.

"Fifty-seven," came a voice from behind us. We turn to see the nurse grinning. She holds her hands up. "I'm not allowed to tell you anything else." She glances up as another team walks in.

We slip out behind them, heading back toward the high school at a walk this time so we could talk strategy.

"This could take hours," I sigh.

"Maybe not," Madi said, ever the optimist. "Think about how many seniors there are. Even split into pairs, some of the water fountains are bound to be in use already."

I guess she was right this time. It only took us searching three fountains before we found the next clue taped to the bottom. I figure that the reason it took so many tries was that other students had already found the clues from the other water fountains.

"I have keys, but no locks and space, and no rooms. You can enter, but you can't go outside." I pause.

A keyboard was the answer, but which one? There has to be hundreds of them in this one building alone. "The computer lab," I say.

Then we rush off to find the correct classroom. That happens to be another homeroom for the seniors. It is the class right next to where we started. Once we make it back to the homeroom classes, we rush in to find notecards once again sitting on each of the desks. Madi snatches up the closest one. I read over her shoulder.

"The ball is flying fast, so you better move past, to find another riddle where you dodged last."

Right then, the bell rings to announce the end of fourth-hour class, and the beginning of lunch for some students. Luckily, though, we are only a couple of halls away from the gymnasium. It takes us a little longer to get there now that we have to make our way through all the other students who are on their way to lunch or their next class. Everyone watches us as we make our way past them, not quite running.

Once we make it to the gym, we find the door frame is once again littered with envelopes. One for each team of two. I take one and read it aloud.

"I am a room, full of rooms, each with a different view. But to enter these rooms, a simple open won't do."

"Room full of rooms? Where is there a room full of rooms inside this school?" Madi asks. "Each with a different view? Stories? The library?"

I shrug and start to head in that direction. Sure enough, as soon as it comes into view, we can see the envelopes taped once again to the door frame. It looks as if there is one for every student, so we both take one.

"Tomorrow is the future, so let us give it a toast. See you tomorrow, we wish you the most." I turn the card over, and the back only says the words "Go home."

I peek into the library, and there is everyone's stuff, stacked into neat piles. We make our way in and collect our things. "Well, that was fun!" I laugh. "Wanna go to the mall?"

That's what we do with our free afternoon. We ride in my car together and spend the entire afternoon going from store to store. We even stop for lunch in between shopping, since we missed it at school.

I drop Madi off at her car before making my way back to my house. I park in the driveway, then look around for the little silver car with the Texas license plates, but not surprisingly, it is nowhere to be seen. Sighing, I gather my bags and head to the front door.

It is not a surprise, not really. They are not here yet. The surprising part is that they are coming at all. Yes, I know they love me, and I love them, but I have so little of them throughout my life. I know almost nothing about them, even though they are my grandparents.

I make my way inside to find my mother sitting on the couch. "Hey mom, I'm home," I called on my way to the stairs. I hear, "Hey baby." I go up to my room just to dump my bags. I then head back down the stairs.

As I come down the stairs, my father is coming out of the kitchen. "Hello Cady, I thought I heard you come in." He has a large bowl of popcorn in his hands and a ready smile on his face for me. "We are going to watch a movie." He smiles at my mother. "Want to join us?"

I am already nodding. "Heck yeah!" I laugh. "What are we watching?"

He chuckles and sits down next to my mother. He then pats the seat beside him. I sit beside him and steal some popcorn as I look up at him.

I have never been sure what features I got from my father, other than my height. He is a six-foot-two-inch lumberjack type of man. He has light brown hair and blue-gray eyes. Completely different from myself.

"It's the one we were talking about last week," he starts. "The one where the world freezes over and the dad travels through the snowstorm to rescue his son and his friends from New York." I get excited. I have wanted to see this one for a while. "We also have a couple more. If we have time."

The first movie we watch in almost silence. The three of us are curled up on the couch eating popcorn and watching the world freeze over.

About two hours later, the end credits rolled.

My father got up to change out the DVD.

"That was good," I tell them. "So worth watching."

"I agree," my mom adds. "I'm not sure why we didn't watch it sooner."

My dad nods. "If that was to happen today," his gaze meets mine, "just know that what that father did, I would do, and so much more if that's what it took to get my baby back."

"Aww dad. I love you too." I smile sweetly at him. "Same, I would do anything I could to keep you both alive and safe."

He gets the DVD put back in its case and holds up two more. On the right is a movie about treasure hunting in the ocean. In his other hand, he holds a movie called *"The Island."*

I look at my mom. She just shrugs. "You pick."

I think about this for a minute. Drug deals and buried treasure, or a fake island with lots of action. I mean, they both have some action, but I point to his left hand.

He gets the film going, then comes back to the couch. While he was messing with the movies, I had moved over to where I was in-between them. I wrap my arms around both of them. "I am really going to miss this quality time with y'all when I leave in a few months."

The instant I speak the words, my father's look of contentedness disappears from his face, and something else replaces it. I cannot figure out what it is though. "College," he sighs.

I drop my arms from around their shoulders and turn to face him a bit more. "What do you mean?"

He exhales again. "Are you sure you want to go to that college?" he inquires. There is something in his tone. Something that is a bit off. There is more to this simple question than I know.

"You know I do. Madi and I have been talking about this for years. You know this too."

He acknowledges that, but there is still something.

"What's wrong with my choice of college?"

He is silent for a moment. I know he is thinking about what he wants to say before it comes out of his mouth. "Nothing," he finally says. He looks over at the TV, then back to me. "Let's just watch the movie, and we can talk about it again later. Let's get through tomorrow first."

I turn back to the movie, but my mood is no longer as bright as it was. The whole conversation with my father is weird. He has not said anything until now. What could be bothering him about this?

I don't know, so I shrug it off and go back to the move. It is actually a really good movie, despite the tension I can feel from my father through the entire thing. Once the movie is over, I leave my parents to clean up the mess we made. I head up to my room. Tomorrow is such a big day; I want to get some sleep.

CHAPTER THREE

Cadence

The sound of the alarm pulls me from the strangest dream the next morning. I am drenched in sweat. I kick off the damp blanket clinging to my sticky skin and sit on the edge of my bed, replaying what details I could remember. Dreams are slippery like that.

I was standing in the front yard, more like a clearing of sorts, in front of an older house. The types you would see in history books. The door to the small house was standing wide open in the biting wind. Snow swirled down in thick, relentless sheets, already blanketing the ground and those gathered outside the small house.

Several others were out there with me in the growing storm. On my side of the clearing, there were four of us total, no coats, and one person without even shoes, as if we'd all rushed out without dressing for the weather. That might have had something to do with the other group standing across from us.

There must have been at least ten of them at first, their presence radiating malice I could feel from where I stood. Another group soon joined, swelling their numbers to fifteen, maybe twenty. They were here to kill every person inside the small house.

That was when the alarm had woken me. So, I did not see the attack, but I have a deep feeling that we were going to die that day, right there in the snow. All the feelings of that dream follow me into the waking world.

I mentally shake myself to get rid of not only the images but the feeling that came along with that strange encounter in dreamland. I did not want to think about that anymore. Not now, or anytime in the future. Unfortunately...we do not always get what we want.

Sitting here, face in my hands, I fell awareness slowly replace the lingering unease until the dream begins to fade. And really, nothing could be better right now, because today is my birthday. I am officially eighteen.

Grinning, I hop up, do a little happy dance, and rush to the bathroom to get ready for graduation.

A while later, I emerge from the steam, wrapped in towels, one around my body, another around my long hair. Being the only one upstairs, I walk to my room without worry, unzipping the garment bag hanging on my closet door. It has been waiting there all week for this day.

Inside was the silver, floor-length gown I'd bought for graduation.

It is mermaid style, with the fabric flaring from the knee into a sweeping tail, the dress hugs my shape from the waist up. One side of the top is strapless; the other has a thick strap to keep everything in place. The silver shimmers against my skin in a way that makes me feel unstoppable.

It is a little too fancy for graduation, maybe, but it is my birthday, and I will wear what I want. I'd fallen in love with it the moment I saw it in the store.

I grab the matching purse and strappy heels on my way out, as well as the bag with my clothes I plan on changing into after graduation.

Everything I needed was already tucked in the bag. Barefoot, I pad downstairs. No point putting the shoes on yet—it would be bad enough wearing them through the whole ceremony.

As I round the corner, the sharp scent of sulfur reaches me, followed by the scratch of a match. My mother stands at the kitchen bar, holding a cupcake with a single lit candle, our tradition since forever.

"Happy birthday, baby girl," she says, smiling. "Make a wish."

I close my eyes, crafting the perfect wish, then blow out the flame.

I take the cupcake from her with a smile on my face. My mother steps back to take in the full view of the dress, and tears start to form in her eyes.

"You look so beautiful." She pauses. "You look so grown up." She leans forward to give me a hug and a quick kiss on the cheek, careful not to mess up my makeup. "I am so proud of you, Cadence." I hold the cupcake out so that she does not smash it between us and ruin this beautiful dress.

"Thanks, Momma." I set the cupcake down on the small plate that was sitting on the countertop and cut it in half before handing half back to her. We eat the cupcake together as we had for the last eighteen years, or as long as I could remember, anyway.

I return her smile. "Thank you again, Mom. I could not have done any of it without you and Dad." I hug her tight. As I pull back, I ask her, "Are you ready to go?"

She nods. I can tell that she was getting emotional, but she is doing a great job of holding it in.

Right then, my father and his parents walk in the front door. My grandmother comes in close and kisses me on the cheek. "Happy birthday, Cadence."

I smile and thank her. I am still marveling at how my father, and his family looks so young. My father is twenty years older than I am. My grandfather is thirty years older than my father, with my grandmother just five years younger than him, but even my grandparents have almost no gray hair.

Grandma's dark blonde hair, almost brown, is always pulled into a sleek bun. I'd never seen it down, so I have no idea how long it is. She shares my father's blue-grey eyes and has only a few faint crow's feet.

My grandfather's light brown hair, just a few shades darker than hers, is streaked with gray at the temples. His brown eyes have fine lines beginning to form, but like hers, they are faint.

Dad checks his watch. "We'd better get going."

My grandfather greets me by way of a side hug and a kiss to the forehead. "Happy birthday, baby." We all make our way outside to the car. My grandfather keeps his arm across my shoulders the entire time, only releasing me as we climb into my mother's car. My grandparents sit in the back seat with me.

We arrive at the school with time to spare. Inside, the gym has big screens that cycles through baby and senior photos of the graduates, each with a short list of accomplishments. We step to the side, waiting for my name to appear.

When the R's started, we watch closely, waiting for my name to appear. When Cadence Robinson flashes on the screen, it displays the pictures I had submitted at the beginning of the year.

My mother's favorite baby picture of me is on the left side of the screen. I must have been about three years old, arms wrapped around a blue pencil prop, wearing a pouty frown. Why that was one of her favorites, I couldn't tell you.

In the center, all my information was on display: name, date of birth, and a long list of the achievements I have earned throughout high school. The information had to cycle twice to get through the list.

On the right is a picture of me sitting on the railing of an old wooden bridge, my favorite. It had been taken last summer in preparation for this very moment. I wore a white summer dress that looked fantastic on me.

Madi has the same picture, just facing the opposite way. If edited together, our photos could be placed back-to-back. We actually did this after having copies made. Each of us has a copy of the edited version in our rooms.

Madi arrives just as the screen moves on to the next student. We make our way back to the band room, where everyone is getting set up. When the time comes, we line up in alphabetical order and wait to enter.

We follow the steps we had practiced so many times: walking down the outer aisles, then through the center, and into the front row where we would sit and wait for our names to be called.

One row at a time stood and waits as their names are announced. While the principal waits for each student, the teachers behind him read off accomplishments and future plans.

Each of us has our picture taken as we receive our diplomas. Then we return to our seats, waiting for the rest of the row to finish before the next row repeats the process.

Once the entire graduating class has received their diplomas, we sit through a few more speeches on stage, longer than the diploma ceremony itself. When it is finally over, we all stand together and toss our caps into the air.

Afterward, the graduating class exits the gymnasium the same way we had entered. Then we each go our separate ways: some back to our families for photos, others moving on to the next celebration. This stage of life is officially complete.

It takes over an hour to pose for all the pictures. Fortunately, I don't mind attention, so many people wants photos with me. Madi and I must take at least a hundred. That's what best friends do.

Now it is time to leave, but all I want is a little more time with my friends. That, however, will not happen; my parents and grandparents have birthday plans for me. I understand. My grandparents are rarely around. Friends could wait. So off I go for family bonding time.

A few hours later, I find myself in a Mexican restaurant uptown, sitting at a table with my parents and grandparents. I have changed out of my beautiful dress into a pair of black low-rise jeans and a white top that doesn't quite meet my jeans, leaving about a two-inch gap of my stomach showing.

We are sitting here talking. We have already ordered and are just snacking on chips and salsa while we all catch up. This seems like a perfect time to ask my mother what I have been thinking about since we left the school.

"Hey, Mom." I take a sip of my tea and raise my eyes to find everyone's gazes now on me. "I have been meaning to ask you why that sad picture of me, when I was little, is your favorite baby picture of me?"

She looks off thoughtful for a minute as if she was remembering the day the picture was taken. "Well, we were doing pictures and everything was going great, but you started to get quiet. Maybe even sleepy, but we only had a few pictures left to take." She smiles at the memory.

"The photographer brought out this blue pencil. It was just plastic, super light and the perfect size for a child your age." She looks back at me.

"You wanted the other toy. I do not even remember now what it was." She breaks off. "You didn't understand what we were doing. You were just about to cry because you wanted the other one. In that moment, I saw you. This sad child sitting there about to cry was all you."

She hesitates. "I wanted that moment captured because not all moments in life are happy, and we need to accept and even embrace all the parts of us, not just the happy moments."

She is quiet for a while. All of us at the table watch her, waiting for her to finish. "And let me tell you, that lady could not have taken a better picture of you. She captured everything I wanted in that moment. It is still my favorite picture of you to this day."

The waiter stops at our table then, with his arms loaded down with plates. He sets everyone's food in front of them, then returns to the kitchen.

As we are eating, my grandmother speaks up. "That is about the time of the 'Great Domino fall' isn't it?"

I look around the table at every one of them because I have no idea what they are talking about. "Great Domino fall?" They all laugh.

"I almost forgot about that," my dad says.

"I could never forget about it." My grandfather rubs his hands down his face, then looks at me. "You were about five or six years old. Your grandmother and I," he pauses to look at her, then back to me, "we had taken you shopping with us on one of our visits. Your grandmother needed to go into a store that you didn't need to be in." I give him a quizzical look, but he doesn't stop his story.

"I decided to go into another store while we waited on Rose." I look around at everyone else to see if they are giving anything away, but no. They are just watching my grandfather tell this story. They all are sharing the mirth. "I was looking at something while you played with the clothes rack beside me."

My grandmother interrupts by placing a hand on Grandpa's arm. "You have to understand how the store was laid out." She smothers another laugh. "The store was set up like stacking Dominos, one rack right after the other. All in long rows that curled into a giant 'S'." They wrapped around the whole store. I know they were trying to display as much as they could in the small space, but still."

My grandfather nods. "I was standing at the third rack inside the door. So, at the beginning of the snake of Dominos. You were playing in the rack beside me. I knew you were there. I was watching you." He chuckles again. "Well, the sales lady comes up and asks me something. I don't even remember what it was now. I turned my back for thirty seconds. It couldn't have been more than that, but in that time, you somehow pulled the rack down, making it bump into the one I was standing beside."

I cover my mouth with my hands because I already know what's coming. He nods. "You got it. The one hit the second and the second hit the third. And so on, until every last one was laying on the ground with its contents spilled all over the floor."

"I wasn't hurt?"

They all crack up again. "No."

I laugh with them and out of the corner of my eye I catch a glimpse of a whole group of employees headed right for our little table. "Oh no!"

The first man that stops at our table smiles at me, then places a sombrero on my head. They all then start singing "Happy Birthday" to me in Spanish. I watch in horror, as the entire restaurant turns to look right at me, as they smash a plate of whipped cream right in my face. Surprising me and causing the table to erupt in laughter. There goes my makeup.

CHAPTER FOUR

Cadence

LATER THAT EVENING WHEN we pull into the driveway, I grab my bag that still holds my dress and other items, and head into the house.

My father must have predicted my reaction because he caught me with a light hand on my arm as my foot hit the first step. "No ma'am," he says. "We need you a little while longer. You can call Madi later." That was exactly what I had planned to do.

I sigh in frustration, but I hang my dress bag on the banister and then turn back toward the living room. I guess he was right again.

"Cadence, please come talk to us," my grandmother requests, though it sounds more like a command. "We'd like to tell you a little more about our family." She pauses, then looks at my mother to include her. "You too, Carol."

I can only imagine the confusion on my face; it must mirror my mother's expression.

"We couldn't tell you before, and you both..." My grandfather cut in, looking at us. "What I'm about to say can never leave this room." He waits until we both nod in agreement. "That also means you cannot tell your friend," he adds, giving me a pointed look.

I shake my head. That might be a dealbreaker. I don't keep secrets from Madi. We tell each other everything. How could he expect me to keep a secret from her, even one I have only just learned? "I mean it, Cadence. This is important."

I am getting more curious by the second. I want to know what this secret is. Maybe this is the reason that they are never around. The question is, do I want to know bad enough to promise to never tell my best friend? I am not sure. I want to know, though, so I reluctantly agree. "I promise."

He nods and takes me at my word. "Now what I am about to say will require you both to keep an open mind, but please let me finish." My grandfather sat on the arm of the chair beside Granny. "Let's begin by saying I have had this conversation many times before, even before your father received a version of the same story on his 18th birthday."

My eyes snap to my father. He knew all this time and hasn't told me. He just shrugs. "You never asked me," he says simply. "I knew they would be coming, and I've heard this story a time or two myself, growing up on the Farm."

I turn to look back at my grandparents. "There is no easy way to say this, so let's just go with the blunt truth. You, my dear Cadence, come from a very long line of shape-shifters."

My mother and I both gasp with disbelief. "What do you mean?" I ask with a light laugh. They must be joking. "Are you telling me I am a werewolf?"

He shakes his head. "A so-called werewolf is just a story. I don't mean there are not any wolf shape-shifters, but they are not called were anything." He put air quotations around the word were. He shakes his head again. "Anyway, we can trace our lineage back thousands of years, back to the original shifters." He looks over at my father, then back at me. "Not every single member of the family, even with a strong shifter gene line, will shift. Some are just carriers, but we will find out tonight if you are a weak carrier or if you will shift. With your mother being human, we are not sure."

"What?" I squeak. "Find out what?" I know he was not being for real. He must be trying to trick me. I look around. "Is this some kind of joke?"

My father answered. "For our kind, on our eighteenth birthday, we either shift for the first time, or we don't shift at all." He smiles bitterly. "I was the latter, the first in our family line in over a thousand years." The disappointment on his face was clear.

"We're not entirely sure what will happen tonight," my granny begins. "With your mother being human and your father unable to shift, we don't know if the bloodline has weakened too much for viable shifter DNA or if it still runs strong enough for you to change."

I shake my head. Why are we even having this conversation? Not that I really believe any of it anyway. "How do we find out?" I ask, trying to humor them. I don't think anything will happen, even if they honestly do believe that it might. It was all nonsense. I jump up out of my seat. "Just tell me what to do!"

"Please sit back down, Cadence." Grandpa looks at his watch, which causes me to look up at the clock on the wall while I did what I was told. It was ten minutes until ten o'clock at night.

"We will leave shortly, but we will have to be outside of town, where no humans will be able to see by midnight." He pauses again. "We need a remote area where, just in case something happens, no one can see. If you do happen to shift, we definitely do not need witnesses."

Grandma stands and walks to the kitchen table, rarely used, and grabs two gift bags I hadn't noticed until now. "One is for tonight, and the other is your birthday present," she says, returning to her seat.

I look at the two bags in front of me. There is one black one and one pink one. The black one was the biggest. The smaller one was pink. Black happens to be my favorite color, and of course it was the biggest, so I pick that one to open first, setting the pink bag on the floor in front of me. Pulling the black bag into my lap, my grandma smiles at my choice but does not say anything.

I pull open the top of the bag, tearing through the small piece of tape that is holding the two flaps together. I open the bag to reveal something black and super fluffy. At first, I think it is a blanket, but as I pull it out, I realize it is a robe. "Oh... This is so soft," I say, rubbing the material against my face. My grandparents smile at each other. They are happy that I like the present.

I put the robe on right over my clothes and reach for the other bag. As soon as I get the package open, I squeal so loud that everyone in the room covers their ears. "A brand-new cell phone!" I jump up to hug them. "The newest BlackBerry! I have been wanting one of these so bad, but Mom and Dad would not buy one."

I return to my seat, reading the box. It is the newest model available. I had wanted a phone but knew I would have to get a job and save up for a good one. Not only for the phone itself but the service as well. My grandparents just saved me the trouble.

My grandfather clears his throat. "Going back to where we were, at midnight, on your eighteenth birthday, if you shift, it will determine what you will be."

I look up at that. "What do you mean?"

"Whatever animal you shift or transform into the night of your birthday is the animal you will always be." He pauses. "What I mean is, if you phase into an eagle like your grandmother, that is what you will be forever."

I nod, so he continues. "Tonight, if you shift, you will not be able to control it. Once you shift, there is no shifting back until the sun rises the morning after, about six hours."

My mother, who had been quiet all this time, starts shouting. "Are you playing some sick joke on me?" She looks around the room. "You all got together and planned to do this to me. Didn't you?"

This must be some form of shock. She had been completely quiet, not even really moving throughout the entire conversation. She was just staring at my grandparents the entire time. I agreed with her to a point, in the beginning. However, now I think it is funny.

I absolutely do not think I am going to turn into a furry animal of any kind, and I do have a lot of disbelief in every single thing they are saying, but on the other hand, if they want to believe that they can turn into animals and fly across the sky, let them. Whatever floats their boat.

My father stands and goes to my mother. He wraps his arms around her, while attempting to comfort her. He leads her into the back of the house toward their bedroom, all the while speaking softly to her.

My grandfather looks back at his watch. "All right, we have to get going soon." They both stand simultaneously. "The robe you received tonight needs to be the only thing you're wearing." He must have seen the look on my face because he held up his hands in front of him. "If you do shift to night, you would tear through any clothing you are wearing or even get tangled in them and potentially get hurt. We don't want that."

"If you want to keep your clothes for now, you can." My grandmother adds. "We can give you some privacy in the car when we get there to change."

I think about it for a second. It is weird, but I can understand what they are saying. If I mysteriously decided to change from a human to some form of animal, then it would probably hurt to have the clothes constricting my body. "Okay, I will keep them for now and change in the car."

They nod, then start for the door on the right, the guest room they normally stay in while they are here. "Give us a minute to change." Is all that was said. Then they disappear, leaving me alone with my thoughts.

Luckily, my parents don't leave me enough time to think over everything that was said. Not even enough time to form any thoughts on the subject. That is probably a good thing. The longer I have to think, the more I would freak.

My mother rushes over to where I am standing. She frames my face with her hands. "Are you okay with all of this?" she asks me; however, I am more worried about her than myself. I just nod. My father is right there beside her, and if he is already on the train to crazy town, I don't want to say anything to offend him. He is still my father after all.

My grandparents did not give me a chance to answer anyway. They come out of the guest room in matching robes. They are thick and fluffy just like mine, but theirs are blue. Each has a small symbol on the left side, up by their shoulder. It looks like an animal howling at the moon, almost like the wolf things you can buy, but that was not a wolf, and it wasn't howling. No, this animal was more elegant. It looks more like a large cat. The moon behind the cat is a beautiful, almost sunset color, but you can still see the details of the craters. "Let's go," he states and walks to the front door. Grandma bends down to pick up a gym bag with the same symbol on it, following her husband.

True to their word, they give me time to remove my clothing when we reached our destination, a wooded area just outside of town. It is dark outside, although with the full moon, there is plenty of light to see to catch up with everyone. We walk into the trees and keep walking for a long time. Just as I am about to ask the most hated question, they come to a stop. I can not see around them, though, so I step up in line with them.

CHAPTER FIVE

Cadence

U P AHEAD, THE TREES thin. Beyond them, I can see a beautiful meadow, with the moon shining so bright we can see everything: the trees, the tall reeds, and even a little creek that runs through the area. "Wow!" I exclaim.

Taking a deep breath of the surroundings, I can smell everything: the richness of the soil beneath the ground, the smell of fresh grass that has to have come from some animal grazing, the smell of the moisture coming from the wet creek that is off to the side, and a whole lot of freshness that you do not get in town.

They just chuckle and walk out into the center of the meadow. "Now Cadence, you will stand here, in the center of this clearing," my grandfather tells me. "We will be over there," he points off in the direction we had just come from, "just inside the tree line. When the time comes, try not to fight the shift. If it does indeed happen, the first time is always the worst, and it will hurt."

I look around once again, taking in the space. "How much longer?"

He glances at the sky, then the ground, and back at me. "Not much longer, about fifteen minutes. You may want to use the robe as a blanket instead of wearing it, but we'll be far enough away that you can."

Everyone comes forward to hug me or kiss my cheek: my mother, my father, my grandparents. Then they move to the spot he had indicated. If I have believed any of this, even a little, I would be completely freaking out. If they just want me to sit here in this beautiful field, surrounded by nature, for no reason other than to enjoy the scenery, I would gladly do it...just to make sure they gave the ticket back.

Once I was alone, I decide to sit instead of stand. I untied the strings around my waist, remove my arms from the holes, but hold onto the lapels, keeping myself covered. I sit down and get comfortable. I am going to be here for a while.

As I wait for nothing to happen, my mind wanders over the past few days. First, my birthday party; I had to do it early with so much going on. It was fantastic, as always. Then the last day of school and graduation. I still can't believe it is real. I am really a high school graduate. In the fall, I'll be going to college with Madi. I still have no idea what I want to study, but I plan to take core classes and figure out the rest later.

Thinking of my best friend, I wish I could tell her what was happening right this minute. But then again, would I really want her to know how crazy my family really is? No, it was probably better this way.

The ground beneath me drew my attention back to my surroundings. A silent vibration began just as clouds covers the moon, plunging the field into darkness.

The vibration turns into a low rumble, making me wonder if an earthquake is happening. I look toward my family, but they show no signs of feeling it.

Just then, the hair starts to stand on the back of my neck. The ground beneath my feet starts shaking harder it feels like an energy of sorts. It kind of feels like a jolt of electricity is slowly making its way, from the ground I now stand on. When did I stand up? What the heck is going on? I was so sure my grandparents had been completely bonkers.

The current, electric feeling, starts to work its way through my feet and into my shins. There is a slight burning to it. I have no idea what was actually going on, but as the current or electricity, whatever it is, starts to travel up my legs, a pain starts to move within my body, following the same path as the electricity. The higher it gets, the more the pain intensifies.

At first, it just feels like my feet has fallen asleep. The little pins and needles that you get sometimes from sitting in the same position for too long. They are just tingly with pinpoints of small pain. As the sensation starts to spread through my legs, whatever it is, the pain intensifies the higher it travels up my body. Starting to burn in places, as if I have stepped into a fire.

Trying to focus on anything but the pain, I look at what should have been my knees. Maybe the pain is causing me to hallucinate, because all I could see in the place of my knees are an uneven set of hairy dog legs.

There is no way that is possible. One is pitch black, with stray strands of gray or white mixed in. The hair is long and shaggy. The other leg is snow white. It is the whitest I have ever seen. This hair, too, is long but smooth. The legs clearly belong to two different animals. They are not the legs I walked into this field on.

The pain is almost blinding. I scream repeatedly, hoping someone will hear me. Can I survive this agony? My entire body feels like it is being incinerated, and there is absolutely nothing I can do; help isn't coming.

Looking down, I think I see a black tail whip past me, but the sight of my stomach draws my attention. Black, short, slick hair is forming before my eyes.

"Holy crap!" I exclaim. I'm not sure if it came out loud or if it is just in my head. I just bought my very own ticket to crazy town because, what the hell —the very same hell my body has been dipped into— is happening to me. Thinking back to the conversation earlier with my grandparents, I was sure they said, or at the very least made it sound like, I would shift into one singular animal. If that were true, why can I see three different hair patterns alone? Let's not even talk about the tail, a freaking tail!

The pain hit a new level. I don't know how much longer I can endure it. I hear a loud crack and scream again. My left arm felt like it just snapped in half, but who can be sure? I collapse onto my side, no longer able to support myself on hands and feet.

I reach up with my right hand to grab the one that just snapped in half, only to find a large paw in the place of my hand. It is bright orange and has black stripes on it, or are those spots? Whirls?

Looking at the arm that should very well be broken, there is nothing but feathers. Where did my hand go?

What the actual hell is going on? I am burning alive on the inside while my entire outside can't make its mind up about what freaking zoo animal it wants to be.

"Oh no!" I try to say, but it only comes out as a grumble. The fire has finally reached my head, and as the pain is so blinding, I can't even think. All I can do is scream, yet no scream emerges. I sound a bit like a wounded bear I had seen at the zoo one year ago.

That is no longer my concern though, because at that point, the darkness starts to creep in, and I have absolutely no desire whatsoever to remain in this pain. I just let the darkness take me away. I will welcome the relief, even if it means death.

Whatever that was that I just went through didn't kill me, though. Because I came to, who knows how long later, with my mother holding my head in her lap, my extremely large head, I might add. She is singing softly to me just like she used to do. Her eyes are red and swollen like she had been crying. I can see my father and grandparents standing nearby talking to one another.

I raise my head to look up at my mother. "Oh, Cady!" she exclaims and hugs my head. I can't understand why there is so much relief mixed with the left-over moisture her face. I had only passed out. The pain had been too much for my brain to process. Now the pain is completely gone like it had never happened. I fell a little weird, but I am all right.

I try to sit up to tell her that, but my body doesn't respond. It is like I can't move. I can lift my head; I know that, but did the pain paralyze me? Did it cause me to be unable to move?

I try a smaller command. Let's see if I can move my arms. I lifted my arm, the one I thought was a wing, but that had to be a hallucination, right? My arm moves on command, and the good thing is there is no longer a single wing on my left side.

Oh no, not a wing. Now there is a huge black paw in the place of the wing and the hand that was originally there. I lift the other hand. At least I matched this time.

Short, slick black fur lined my hands and arms, each ending in five wickedly sharp claws. I play with them for a moment to understand their movement. Looking down my body, I see the same black fur, and, of course, the freaking tail is still there.

I get a great idea. Rolling off my mother, I get to my paws. I had to think as if I am walking on hands and knees, and it works. I am not paralyzed after all! After a few minutes of learning to move as a huge cat, I make my way over to my parents.

"All right, baby," my mother says. "Now that I know you're okay, we're going home. You'll have to stay here, of course, but we'll be back at dawn." She leans down to kiss my big head. "Love you, honey." She took my father's hand and walks back toward the car.

I turn to my grandparents. Neither spoke; they shift right there in front of me, letting their robes fall to the ground. I watch them transform seamlessly from humans to animals. I wonder what had gone wrong with my shift. They each became a single animal, not the whole dang zoo.

"Well... we did not expect this," my grandfather's voice sounds in my head. He can't speak aloud because he is now a tiger, a normal-sized one. I could rest my head on top of his if I was brave enough.

In my grandmother's place, now sits an eagle. She looks a little big, but who was I to judge? It's not like I have ever seen one of those up close before. Maybe it was normal.

My grandfather turns and starts to walk away, but not before my grandmother flies up to rest on his back. With her wings outstretched, she looks a lot like my hallucination. "*It seems that we might need to tell you another story, one that we thought was just a legend at this point."*

I look him over and wonder if they could read my thoughts or if I must do something different to speak to them. *"Can you hear me?"* I ask, testing it out.

My grandmother chuckles in my head, chirping aloud. That is a weird sensation; my mind and ears are telling me different things. *"Yes, Cadence, we hear you. In our animal forms, we speak telepathically to other shifters only. We cannot hear each other's thoughts, and we cannot speak to humans."*

"All of it, including the zoo I went through to get here." I pause, looking down in shame. *"I really thought you were crazy."*

"We knew you didn't believe us. You broadcast it loud and clear, facial expressions and eye rolls included." Even as a bird, I understand her. *"We simply chose to wait and see what would happen."*

"As for the zoo, as you called it," my grandfather interrupts. *"That question is different. We don't know. We only know that you must be the Black Dawn, the shifter of legends."*

Before I can freak out, my grandmother adds, *"This form alone is new. There has only been one black panther since the first shifter. You are the first since then. That is why we suspect you are the Black Dawn."* She emphasizes the title and looks up at the still-clouded moon.

"I have only heard the story a few times myself, so some of the details may have been lost or unclear, but I will tell you what I do know, and later, when we are more ourselves, we can find out more." She looks back at me. *"We have always been told that when the greatest of all our power is born, there will be a black dawn."* She looks around again. *"The night sky will darken, and there will be a lunar eclipse."*

"The Black Dawn is the marking that shows all other shifters that our great leader has joined us. The great leader will once again bring peace to our people so that we can once again be the protectors of the humans." He looks back at my grandmother since they are taking turns telling me this, not giving me a chance to think or freak.

"You are our queen, according to legend. When this lunar eclipse is over, your shape will appear. Shifters everywhere will know our great queen, or king, has been born, and they will watch to see who, or what, you are." She pauses. *"I guess it's good a cat cast in shadows could be any type of cat. That will help us keep you safe."*

I start to shake my head. *"What does all that mean? Black Dawn, lunar eclipses, keeping me safe?"* This cannot be happening right now. I start to pace back and forth in front of them. I am just now able to even move around in this form, and it sounds like they want me to drop everything and go lead people I have never met and know almost nothing about. Maybe they still are crazy.

My grandfather steps in front of me, stopping my pacing. Even smaller than me, I could feel his power. *"Let's not worry about it tonight. Let's just run, play, and let our animals free for a while. We'll figure out the details later."*

That's exactly what we did. We ran until I was tired, played in the creek, and even took a nap. As dawn approached, we return to the center of the field where we had left our robes. My grandparents change back in the trees and rejoin me in the clearing.

CHAPTER SIX

Cadence

J UST AS WE CAN start to see the first glimpse of light and color from the sun rising, the moon decides to take a vacation. It goes completely dark, almost as if it just disappeared right from the sky. For several long moments, absolute darkness fills the space all around us.

I cannot even see my grandparents, even though I know for a fact that they are standing right next to me. It looks as if all of the light in the world has been sucked into a dark hole somewhere deep in space. I cannot even see the stars through the darkness.

All at once, the blackness starts to shrink in on itself, as if it is being sucked into the center or being given back to us only in shades of orange. When there is just a small black spot left in the center, several things happen at once, making me wonder what really happened first.

The speck explodes into a ball of light so bright I have to close my eyes to avoid burning my retinas. When the brightness fades behind my lids, I finally open them. The sun is rising over the horizon, and the moon reveals a familiar sight: a large cat howling at the moon, a blood moon behind it, just like the symbol on my grandparents' robes.

I only get a glimpse because my body decides to take control once again. The fire I had felt before returns, engulfing me entirely, without giving me a chance to breathe. It goes from nothing to what I can only imagine stepping into a campfire would feel like. The pain is so instant that I do not even feel my body shifting back to human form. I only know it has happened because, when the pain disappears, I am no longer an animal; I am lying in a fetal position, naked as the day I was born.

Once I am fully human again, I just lay there trying to get my body to recover. It doesn't matter that I was naked. At this point, I don't even care. At some point, though, I feel something being draped over my naked body, only covering the important bits. I think it's my new robe, but who could be sure? When I had it on before, it was soft and fluffy; however, now it feels itchy and rough. I want nothing more than to throw it off. I would, too, but I still can't move.

After several long minutes, I am able to move once again. I slip my arms back into the robe, tie the sash, and sit up slowly. I look around, and my father has arrived at some point while I was lying here helpless. He is standing next to my grandparents. I do believe they are talking about me. The looks they are giving me say it all.

I slowly come to my feet, adjusting the robe. "That..." I try to speak, but it comes out broken and raspy, like I have been smoking for decades. "That was rough." I clear my throat and try again. My grandmother steps in front of me.

"It always is the first time, though yours looked worse than normal for a shifter, for some reason." She smiles apologetically.

My skin is still super sensitive; the robe just feels wrong on my skin. For modesty's sake, I keep it on. "Would it have anything to do with the mixed-up zoo I changed into?" I ask. "I thought you said I would be one animal." I look at them accusingly.

She frowns. "We really don't know." She glances at my grandfather. "We've led the Central Region for forty years, and until today, we've never seen anything like what you just went through."

The men join us. "For the average shifter, their first shift is long and painful, sometimes taking hours, caught between human and animal," my grandfather says. "The shortest shift I've ever seen lasted about an hour."

My grandmother places a hand lightly on my shoulder. "I know it may feel longer, but you went through the entire zoo in less than twenty minutes, the fastest initial shift ever recorded."

I start to sway, the fatigue catching up to me quickly. My father notices, then starts to herd us to the cars. "Unfortunately, you will not be able to sleep just yet." My grandfather states. "We need to have another conversation that you are not going to like."

I laugh bitterly. "You think I like any of this?" Who knew, when I had been so excited a few days ago, that I would be now, wishing for the first time in my life that I could have had a different family? I love my life, and I love my parents dearly, but I don't want to be this person.

Once my father begins driving us home, my grandfather continues. "I know you don't, but we can't control fate. You, my dear granddaughter, are the fate of every shapeshifter alive." He pauses, looking at me. "I'm sorry to put this on your shoulders, but our enemies are drawing closer, and time is running out."

I am not sure who he thinks I am, but I am no one's saving grace. I am just Cadence Robinson, an eighteen-year-old, fresh out of school, and I don't even know enough about the human world to try to save anyone. Now he wants me to go save a species that I didn't know existed until a few hours ago. "No, thank you."

I have plans. Those plans do not include anyone but myself and my best friend. Going to college is important to me, but being with Madi is even more important. "What are you saying anyway? What are you expecting me to do?"

My grandmother takes my hand in hers and looks me right in the eyes. "We need you do come back with us to Texas. We need you to train to become our leader. I don't want to take you away..."

"No way." I rip my hands away from her. "I'm not going anywhere. I have my life planned out and it does *not* include this."

"We need you." My grandfather states matter-of-factly. "You do not understand this, but without you, our entire race will die. She will kill us all." He stopped briefly. "You included."

"Cady, please, just give it a chance," Dad cut in. "Try it out for a few months. If you decide that you still don't want to help, then you can come home and go on with your plans."

My grandfather starts to speak, but Dad stops him. "No, Dad. This must be her decision. We cannot force her."

My grandmother agrees. "Yes, honey. You come with us for three months. If you still want to go home then, we'll let you." She smiles. "Even if you do, by then, you'll have the skills and knowledge to protect yourself and your family."

My family? Was she implying that if I didn't do this, my parents and friends like Madi would be at risk? I can't let that happen. There is no way I will let that happen.

Three months isn't long; I could train and still be back for college. I would do it, for their sake. "Okay. Three months, and if I want to return, I can." I agree, just as Dad pulls into our driveway.

My mother is standing outside waiting for us to get back. I am not sure why she didn't go with Dad to pick us up. Before the car was even out of gear, she was already trying to open my door.

"Oh, baby, I was so scared for you." She pulls me out of the car and wraps me in a tight hug. My sensitive skin is still raw, so it makes me wince, but I hug my mother back with the same amount of force. The time with my mother is worth the pain.

I know this move, even for only three months, will be hardest on her. So, I let her hold me, enduring the screaming of my skin. I won't let anything happen to my sweet mother.

When she finally pulls back, I hold in a sigh of relief. She wouldn't understand, and I don't want to hurt her feelings.

The relief doesn't last long; she starts patting my head and arms, even turns me around to check my backside.

"Are you okay?" she asks hesitantly. "All of the... extras gone?"

I laugh. "Yes, Mom. I'm fine now. The entire zoo is gone, maybe forever, I don't know. It's gone for now, though."

We start to go inside. This conversation needs to be behind closed doors.

Once inside, I stop in my tracks. The suitcases she had bought for last year's vacation were off to the side of the entryway, all five of them full. My purse sat atop them. My eyes go straight to my mom. "You know?"

"Your father explained it all to me. I'm sad, but I know you must go."

I look at my father, thinking he must have just found out ten minutes ago.

He winks at me. "I grew up on the Farm," he chuckles. "I've heard the stories myself a time or two."

I shake my head and open my mouth to speak, but my grandfather interrupts me before I can respond. "We also need to get on the road soon," he says, looking at his watch, which must have been put back on in the car. "We have a long trip ahead of us."

I am upset that I don't have any longer with my parents or even a chance to call my best friend. I just wish I had time for a nap, a really long nap.

My grandfather goes to take my bags to the car while the rest of us say our goodbyes. "I love you, Cady-Did." Mom says, wrapping me in another tight hug. It is only for three months. We could do this. I hug my father and climb into my grandparents' car.

Once we are on the interstate, I lay down in the back seat. If I don't lie down soon, I am going to pass out again, and that is the last thing I want for an exceptionally long time. It isn't the act of passing out; it is the fact of losing time. That bothers me on a level I don't even understand myself.

What feels like five minutes later, I wake up as my grandfather is pulling up to a gas pump. I sit up and rub my eyes. "Where are we?"

My grandmother looks up from her book. "Right outside Texarkana," she says, placing a bookmark and closing the book. "We're just stopping for gas, and a potty break, if you need it."

Half an hour later, we are back on the road, my grandmother driving this time. It doesn't take long for me to fall asleep again. When I wake, I feel more rested. It felt like I'd slept for hours; the car's display indicated ten. "Holy crap!"

"The first shift is always like that," my grandmother tells me as she takes an exit off the highway. She had to have known what I was referring to. "Believe it or not, you will be able to sleep again as soon as we get to the Farm, but you might want to put your clothes on now," she laughs.

I glance down at myself to see I am still wearing the black robe and naked as a jaybird underneath. The robe has shifted sideways, revealing a whole lot of skin. I make a sound and grab the lapels, straightening up the mess I am wearing. My grandmother just laughs again. Nudity is nothing new to shape-shifters, apparently.

Looking straight ahead, my grandfather gives me some privacy to dress. The clothes from the night before are still in the seat beside me, wrinkled from my sleeping on them, but they will have to do. "It's a good thing you're up," he says as I slipped into them. "We need to talk before we get there."

Once I finish, he turns to me. "It's particularly important to keep your identity a secret. We don't want anyone finding out who you are before you get training."

I can understand that, to a point. If I really am the only person who can save the shifters, then I will be more valuable dead. I definitely don't want to be dead.

"Normally, I would say that those at the Farm could be trusted, but we have a few guests." My grandfather looks back at me. "There are two delegates from each of the other areas, which is one reason we had to rush home. In three days, we will be having our quarterly summit meeting." He looks back at the road in front of him.

"The leaders of the other regions will be coming, and we don't want them to know who you are. So, we have a favor to ask: for the next few days, we would like you to lay low. No shifting in the sight of others. Avoid telling anyone who you are. That kind of thing. Once everyone from the summit is gone, we can try to find a new normal."

"Tomorrow morning, I'll call in Hunter, our trainer for anything big-cat related," my grandmother says, taking her turn in their storytelling way.

"We can start your training in secret once he arrives." She pauses. "Oh, I almost forgot, we'd like you to keep the birthmark on your back covered."

I love my birthmark, but it makes sense now. Between my shoulder blades is a patch of discolored skin in the shape of a cat. It is one of the really unique features about me. Normal birthmarks didn't have much substance, but mine does.

I don't get a chance to respond; the car pulls up to a large gate, at least ten feet high, topped with barbed wire at least four feet deep. A sign warns of high-voltage electricity.

She stops the car at the building that sits beside the gate. She rolls down the window.

"Welcome home, Rose and Robert," the man says as he stands in an open window.

"Who do we have here?" he leans down to see me in the back seat. I was sure glad I got my clothes back on now.

Rose, AKA my grandmother, smiles at him. "This is my granddaughter, Cadence. She will be staying with us for a while." The man's smile got bigger. He looks to be in his thirties with dark blonde hair.

"Nice to meet you, ma'am." He says, then presses a button beside him.

The gate swings open, allowing us entrance into... A forest. There is nothing but trees beyond the gate. I can't even see a path, but Granny must know where it is because she just glides right between two trees.

CHAPTER SEVEN

Cadence

I WATCH AS WE pass nothing but trees. For the longest time, I don't even see the path, but Granny knows exactly where we are going.

Before long, I can make out objects ahead through the now-thinning trees. We pass through the last of the forest and enter a large open space. From here, I can see at least a couple of acres of cleared land, right in the center of the forest.

Several cars are parked around a circular drive, and a parking lot sits to the right of the pathway leading to the circular drive and the house beyond. Further to the right, there is a massive building with large bay-style doors; I assume it is a garage, albeit an enormous one.

Then I turn my attention to the house itself...

Well, it is shaped like a house, mostly, a long, tall house, but there are towers on each side that look to have at least three stories.

The main, central part of the house is white with brown trim work, which appears to be in a pattern.

Not sure what the pattern is for, but it looks cool. Each of the princess towers are made of brick. The windows are arched, giving the entire house a fairy-tale feeling. I could see there is a basement, but I am unsure of much else.

There are people everywhere. As we get out of the car, several of them rush forward. Some go to the trunk, and others greet my grandparents. Everyone stares at me, but no one is as forthcoming with their questions as the man at the gate. I am too busy looking around to care. I am used to attention, so this is nothing new.

There is so much to see. In every direction I turn, there is something else to look at. I am not even paying attention to anything that is being said around me, but I'm afraid that I have been called several times because when I finally hear my name, my grandfather's voice was so loud that several people around me just stop and stare, some even lowering their heads.

I quickly look up to find that they are several feet in front of me. I am so busy looking at everything new that I completely miss myself getting left behind in a brand-new environment. I would have found my way eventually. At least it would have given me time to explore.

I hurry to catch up, muttering an apology as I reach them. I need to pay more attention; I can't get left behind again, not so soon after arriving.

Everyone around us remains quiet as we walk toward the arched doorway. A small crowd follows us. I try to focus, but when we enter the first set of arched doors, I find an outdoor seating area on each side of the entrance.

After everything I had already seen since we passed through the front gate, I thought I was prepared to walk through those doors, but I was nowhere near prepared to completely step back through time. There is so much of a difference that I turn around to look back through the open doorway to make sure I had not, in fact, discovered time travel.

Have you ever wondered what it would be like back in the olden days? Where people are classed by whatever? To live in one of the old-style houses, doing just what they did back then? Well, not me. I like living in the here and now, but I can still appreciate a well-built house.

The inside of the house was made to draw you into the time that it was built. My guess is that the entryway was at least from the 1700s, with classics of that time. The beautiful pine wood floors and ornate woodworking open into beamed ceilings.

There is what looks like an original fireplace right in the center of the room. The fireplace is framed by staircases that curve around up to a landing on the second floor. From here, I can see some sort of sitting area.

Two doorways lead off to each side of the room, and what appears to be halls that lead behind the stairs. This is truly a statement piece of an entryway that —at the time and still today— screams wealth. I personally am not new to wealth, but this is over the top.

"Come along now," Granny says and leads us down the hall to the left of the fireplace. "Please come into the conference room." She leads me down the hall, and behind the fireplace, there is a door. She steps in and closes the door behind us as soon as we are inside.

"This room is soundproof. Anything said in this room will not be overheard by others." She sits at one of the two chairs at the head of the table and points to the chair to her left, the one on the side of the table. "Sit here, please."

Once I am seated, she starts again. "This is where the summit will be held. As well as any conversations that relate to your status."

She pauses and tilts her head thoughtfully. "A summit in this context refers to a meeting that is held by the area leaders every three months."

Before I have a chance to say anything in return, the door opens on the other side of the room. My grandfather and another couple walks in. My grandfather takes the seat next to Granny. The couple come and sits on the opposite side of the table from me.

"Cadence, this is Jameson and Emily Foster," he points to the couple. "When your grandmother and I cannot be here, they are in charge. Guys, this is my granddaughter Cadence Robinson."

The man sitting next to my grandfather has almost the same skin tone and hair as I do, but he has honey-brown eyes. I can tell that he is tall when he came in. I'm not sure how tall, but he has to be over six feet. His large, honey-colored, brown eyes are piercing in a way that would make you think he could see to your very soul.

The female has almost the same eyes, only her cat-like eyes are more mysterious. Her skin is almost milk chocolate. She appears to be more trusting than the male. She has deep brown hair that is pulled up into a tight bun. Each offers a hand to shake as they are being introduced.

My grandfather waits until we finish shaking hands, then he drops the bomb.

"The Black Dawn..." Their eyes widen, and both of their jaws almost hit the table. My grandfather laughs. I have never seen my grandfather this playful with anyone other than my family, but then again, I have never seen him with anyone other than my family.

Once he recovers, he cleared his throat. "In all reality, yes, she is the new queen, but no one can find out, and with that, I will need your trust and help."

They straighten. Their faces go right back to impassive before the male, Jameson, speaks; however, he is still staring at me. "Whatever you need, sir."

"Alright now." My grandfather clears his throat and looks back at me. "We talked a little about the summit. We didn't get a chance to go into many details. Let us start out by saying that there are five different regions. Central..."

He looks around before coming back to me. "... is where we are now. Then one region for each cardinal direction. North being Alaska. South is Hawaii. Each region has a leader or a set of leaders." He points to himself and my grandmother. "They will all be here for the summit. The ones we need to watch the most would be from the East Region. Tony is the leader of the East. He is from New York. We believe him to be using shifters for the mob, but we cannot prove it. Every shifter that we have sent into investigate was either returned in a body bag or switched sides."

"Not that any of the leaders are pushovers, or they wouldn't be in their positions. Tony is the worst. So... we want you to see if you are willing to play mouse for the time that the delegates are here and through the summit. I know that is against your nature, but the rewards outweigh the risk."

If that was all she is going to ask me to do for the time being, I would definitely try. At the end of the day, I am still just trying to protect my parents and Madi. "I cannot make any promises, but I will promise to try my best."

She nods. "That is all that we can ask. Now it is late. We will meet back here in the morning..." She was interrupted by the sound of a doorbell.

"Perfect timing."

A young girl, not much younger than me, opens the door. She wears a navy-blue uniform, shirt and pants, with the same cat-and-moon symbol I'd seen everywhere. Under the symbol, 'staff' is printed in white letters.

"You called for me, ma'am?" she asks timidly.

Granny smiles. "Yes, Anna. Please come in." The girl steps fully inside and closes the door.

Once inside, I get a good look at her. She is small, exactly as Granny had described, mousy. No more than five feet tall, with a slight frame making her appear younger. Short brown hair cut into a bob stopping at her shoulders. Standing before me, she could have passed for thirteen. Her eyes are downcast, so I can not see much else.

"I'd like you to show my granddaughter to her room and help her with anything she needs," Granny instructs, then turns to me. "Cadence, this is Anna Moore. She works here at the Farm. She will be your guide." Granny gave me a look that made me feel I could trust her.

The girl nods enthusiastically. "Yes, ma'am." She smiles shyly at me, then turns toward the door. "Right this way, please."

I look at the girl, then back to my grandparents, and they both nod at the same time. "Go get settled. Even though you slept in the car, you will soon crash again." She pats my hand softly. "It always happens."

She then turns to Anna. "Please come back and see me once you are finished." The girl inclines her head before turning back to me.

I did what I was told. I joined the small girl in the hall. I stand at least a foot taller than her. "Right this way, please." She said again, then walked out the door. I followed her.

She doesn't say anything else, simply leading the way to the entryway and up the left side of the stairs. When she reaches the last door on the long hall, she stops, opens it, and steps back.

"I put your things in here as instructed," she says with a small smile, this time a bit bigger.

"Thank you." I pause, wondering if I should strike up a conversation.

"Granny said your name was Anna?" She nods. "How old are you?"

"I'm two weeks past my eighteenth birthday, ma'am," she says hesitantly. I can tell she doesn't like sharing this information. She probably gets asked this all the time given her size. I'm not being mean; I am simply curious.

I smile, trying to remember my part and be myself at the same time.

"Please don't call me ma'am... I am nowhere near old enough to be called ma'am. I am just Cadence, or you can call me Cady. No ma'am is needed." I smile. "I would love it if we could be friends." Leaving all my friends behind in Missouri is hard. It will be even harder if I don't have any here.

That adjusts her attitude a little. "I am sorry, but it is ingrained in me that I must. Still, I will adjust. Yes, I would love to be friends."

I shake my head. "I am just a regular girl, your own age. I don't want special treatment. I just want to be treated like everyone else." I address the first half of her sentence.

"But... I need my job." She stops herself, pauses, and then tries again. "Alright, but in public, I must do my job; however, while we are alone, I will do as you ask."

"Good enough for me." I turn to walk into the room. "Goodnight, Anna."

As the door closes behind me, I take in the sight of my new room. There is a king-size canopy bed sitting in the center of the room with a padded bench at the foot of the bed. There is a tall chest of drawers sitting opposite the bed. There are also two doors that lead somewhere. I assume one would be a closet, where hopefully my bags are, and one would be the bathroom.

I pick one at random. Turns out, door number one is a bathroom. Since I am not ready for that yet, I go to door number two. Bingo, the closet with my bags, but it looks like Anna had already been here first. My clothes are already hanging in the closet. She works fast.

I grab a set of pajamas, then go straight back to door number one. I shower as quickly as possible. My grandmother had been correct once again. By the time I am finished showering, it feels like I haven't slept in a week. I head to the bed, not even bothering to get dressed.

By the time I wake again, it is already bright outside. The clock on the bedside table reads almost eleven in the morning. I must have needed another twelve hours of sleep.

I walk naked into the closet and pick out jeans and a black T-shirt, remembering what I'd been told about my birthmark. The only way to cover it without a hoodie is a basic T-shirt. Once dressed, I plan to find my grandmother, then get something to eat—definitely food first. My stomach growls to second that priority.

I walk out of my bedroom door to find Anna walking down the hall. "I was just coming to wake you," she tells me in greeting. "Rose would like to see you." I nod, and I guess I will be seeing Granny before food.

"I've been asked to inform you that the delegates are in the right hall." She looks slightly confused, probably wondering why she needed to tell me that. I am not about to enlighten her.

She leads me back to the soundproof room behind the fireplace.

I walk in to find my grandmother alone in the room. She is sitting in the same chair as yesterday. In front of her, there are a bunch of papers. There is now also a landline phone that she just so happens to be holding to her ear.

"Yes, I understand, dear," she waves me in. "Alright, I will see you then." She hangs up the phone, then turns to look at me.

"Good morning."

I take a seat next to her; I know it is my grandpa's seat, but I sit in it anyway. She doesn't say anything about it.

"Good morning, Granny. You wanted to see me?"

"Well, originally, we were going to call Hunter, a tiger shifter that is currently in the northern region, but he is not available," she pauses. "I didn't really want to use anyone else, but I called Nathan. I guess we will just have to be careful."

My stomach growls again, reminding me that it needs attention, but I ignore it. "When do we start?" Even though I ignored the growling in my stomach, my grandmother did not fail to take notice. I laugh. "Well, it would be good to eat first."

She looks down at my stomach as it makes itself known again. "You have a couple of hours. Eat, and have Anna give you a quick tour."

She didn't have to tell me twice. "Okay, love you." Old habits die hard.

I rejoin Anna out in the hall. I find her leaning against the wall, staring off into space. I tend to do that myself when I am thinking about something. "I need food badly," I tell her as my stomach growls again.

"Me too," she agrees." Right this way." She leads me back to the entryway, which I am learning is the pathway to all doors. She walks around the fireplace to another set of doors.

I follow her in the doorway, and I am instantly assaulted by so many smells that it makes my stomach sound off again, making me think I haven't eaten in ages. She goes straight to the buffet that is set up, not even noticing that I have stopped just inside the door. There are just too many lovely smells coming into the room that I have no choice but to stop and take it all in.

The room is a basic dining area, though there are no standard tables, at least none that are not covered. A long buffet-style table with warmers line the far side of the room, steam rising from the food. Bacon is the most prominent aroma.

Several smaller tables are spread throughout, each loaded with water bottles, soda, chips, and fruit. There is an abundance of food. Two doors on the right side of the room, one in each corner, made three entryways total. One leads outside.

Anna grabs two plates and hands me one. She waits for me to go ahead of her. Her training is evident. With so many options on the buffet, I just stand, taking it all in. A sign indicates custom orders are available upon request.

I fill my plate with some of my favorite foods, picking up silverware and a drink. I step aside to wait for Anna, unsure of where she plans to go.

Once she has her food, she turns to the door leading outside. "I normally eat outside when I can. Do you mind?" I shake my head and follow her.

Chapter Eight

Hunter

"ARE YOU COMING TO Frankie's moonlight ceremony?" my trainee asks as we step out into the bitter cold. In May, temperatures still hover around freezing. Alaska has always felt cold to me.

I look over at the lynx shifter. I'd been training him and a few others for about six months now here at the Northern Region headquarters. I will be so happy when this week was over. Three more days, and my self-appointed rotation in the Northern Territory, stationed in Alaska, would finally be done.

The moonlight ceremony the lynx mentioned was for the leader of this territory's son. The day before I leave Alaska for the Western Territory and its sunny California skies... maybe even the Southern Territories of Hawaii.

As a nomad, I belong to all territories and am free to travel wherever I choose. Except east, but anywhere else, I'm welcome. Wherever I go, I help train new shifters, all in the quest to find her.

"Hunter?" Steven, the lynx, asks, as if this wasn't the first time I have missed him speaking.

"Sorry, what?" I stop in my tracks and face him.

He laughs. "That's what I thought," he says, starting to walk again, and I fell in step beside him. "I asked if you were going to Frankie's moonlight."

I nod. "Yes, I plan to be there. I don't leave until the next morning, so I'll pay my respects." I look over at him. "You better not slack off on your training once I'm gone either," I warn.

He just chuckles. "I would not do that, now would I?"

I laugh with him.

"Yes, you would, but if you are ever needed for a real battle, you have to stay at your best." We enter the training field. "I did not freeze my balls off for the last six months for you to die in your first real battle." I pause as we take off our jackets. "Now let's get to work."

I set off at a steady jog. He is soon right beside me. After the first couple of laps, I increase our speed. We run for the next half hour before slowing down. After the cooldown time, we have been running for an hour. This is how we start every training session.

I return to my room to shower before heading down to lunch. After lunch, we are back at it again. We go through the same routine as we have every day for the last few months.

Running, cardio, push-ups, sit-ups, and shifting. We did this three times a day. Every day. Steven is starting as a guard this weekend, part of the defense team for the area leaders.

He needs to be in top shape, and he is. I had made sure he is. He did not know it yet, but this is our last intense training session. The next two days flew by. We run only in the mornings, and I give him the rest of the days off, just so he could get a break before the real work began.

On my last night in the Northern Territory, I find myself following about a dozen people who were invited to watch Frankie's moonlight ceremony. We gather around the edges of the training field.

When these ceremonies are made public, the guests gather around, keeping enough of a distance to give the immediate family privacy, both to show respect and honor the shifter in the center.

Once the shifter transforms, the gathered group would change with him and then run alongside the new shifter. When they return to human form at dawn, everyone would go home to sleep.

I glance at my watch. Only five more minutes. Frankie is already in the center of the training field, with only his parents inside the ring. Around thirty others stand along the field's edges. I join the observers.

With his parents being different shifter types, Frankie could change into either one. His father is a lynx, just like Steven, and his mother is some type of bird; I am not sure which.

I glance up as a cloud drifts away, revealing a beautiful moon. Its rays shine down on the gathered group, and Frankie let out a yip that draws my attention. He drops to all fours. As his body begins to change for the first time, we hear him scream. Feathers appear along his arms as his form shrinks. It takes him nearly an hour to complete the full transition from human to raven. When he finished, he collapses on his side, panting.

When he stands again, the crowd cheers and begins to shift. We run, played, and chased one another as a group for the rest of the night. As the sun started to rise, we all turned back toward the training field. Then, suddenly, the world went black.

I looked up at the sky; the others around me were doing the same. For several moments, we were plunged into darkness. Complete darkness. I heard murmurs all around me, but I just watched.

This was too big a moment to miss something because I looked away. We have all heard the stories. Just as quickly as it started, the darkness begins to shrink away, pulling back in on itself. As the darkness drew into itself, right in the center of the moon, it seems to explode.

The explosion sends an extremely bright light in every direction. Going from complete darkness to supernova bright has every single one of us jerking our heads down for a moment, closing our eyes against the brightness.

When the light fades and I can no longer feel the brightness behind my closed eyelids, I open my eyes. I look back up to see that the sun has moved, but there is now a shape in the light of the moon, a large cat.

The lunar eclipse that we have been waiting hundreds of years for. I am not the only shifter in this field who knows what this means.

"Oh my God!" I hear next to me.

"The Black Dawn."

"Finally!" So many voices, and all I could do is stare in awe.

The image did not last long. Seconds after the sun slid out from behind the moon, the cat is gone. If you were not watching, you would never have known it happened.

Legends of the Black Dawn, the greatest among us, had been told for centuries. Most of us believed them to be nothing more than stories. But any shifter who witnessed what we just had would know the truth: they were real, and whoever they were, they had just been reborn into this world.

After the night's events, I decide to remain in the Northern Region for a few more days. Franklin has meetings all day, calling in favors and trying to gather any information he could about the Black Dawn. So far, he hasn't found any solid evidence.

We were in yet another meeting when my phone rings. I step into the hall to answer the call from the Central Region leaders.

"Hello," I greet.

"Hello, Hunter. This is Rose from the Central Region." I nod, even though she couldn't see me.

"Yes, ma'am. How can I help you?" I ask.

She is probably seeking information just like the rest of us. Information that we do not have. She clears her throat. "I will get straight to the point. I need a trainer. I would rather have you if that is possible, since you are the best."

So, it is not information she was after. I do not want to lie to her, but once I am finished here, I plan to take a vacation. I must have my downtime. It was one of the most important aspects of what I do. That is how I am as good as I am. A reset of sorts.

"I'm currently in the middle of something, ma'am, and I can't get away." That is mostly the truth.

I hear a disappointed sigh on the other end. Rose is frustrated, but that is her problem. I can't help her right now.

"That's unfortunate. Well, thank you for your time. If anything changes, please let me know."

"Will do." I end the call and return to the meeting.

CHAPTER NINE

Cadence

SHE LEADS ME TO a table that already has a few people sitting at it. There is still plenty of room for the two of us.

"Hey, guys," Anna greets, then sits down. I slide in next to her. She points to each person around us and begins introducing them.

I guess she isn't as hungry as I am. I start eating even as she talks; it has been too long, and shifting twice has burned a lot of energy. I can't wait.

She points to the only female. "This is Mackenzie. She's new here too."

I smiled at the girl but didn't speak; I was too busy shoveling food into my mouth.

She is about our age with super curly dark brown hair, not the kind you get from those little boxes at the store. Her hair is the most beautiful shade of brown, shoulder-length and perfectly curly. I have no idea how it isn't a frizzy mess, but it is glossy and staying perfectly in place.

She looks friendly even before she smiles. When she does, it lights up her gorgeous brown eyes. She waves at me, noticing I am still eating. I swallow quickly before greeting her. "Hello, Mack." I shorten her name, and she smiles even bigger. "I'm Cady." I go back to eating; shifting was hungry work.

By then, Anna has started eating. She pauses to point to the male beside Mack. He looks a lot like the girl next to him; except he has short hair, and his skin is a bit darker than his sisters. If I was a betting girl, I would have to put money down that they are twins.

"This is Adam, Mackenzie's twin," Anna confirms. I would have won big with that one. He smiles and waves, letting me continue eating.

The last person at the table is a blonde. He looks a few years older than the rest of us, maybe a couple of years. Black-framed glasses highlights the suspicion in his blue eyes, and a few acne scars mark his face.

"This is Travis." He doesn't wave or look my way, acting as if I am not even there.

All right then. I shrug and go back to my food. Travis looks up, thinking I am not paying attention. He has a sneer on his face. I meet his eyes mid-eye roll.

"You got a problem?" I ask straight, forgetting I'm supposed to be meek. This is harder than I thought it would be. And this is only day one.

He doesn't answer, just looks away with a look of disgust.

"Ignore him," Mack says. "I don't know what his problem is. So, tell us about you."

Once I finish the last bite, Anna gathers our plates and takes them inside.

"What do you want to know?"

"Where are you from?" I ask.

She looks at her brother, then back to me. "We're from Florida. It's a good thing too, or this heat would kill us. It's still different, though."

I nod. The little time I have been outside is already making me sweat. "I live..." I pause, thinking carefully. I know I am only staying here for three months, so I am not sure whether to say "live" or "lived." "...in Cape Girardeau, MO." I look at Anna, who is just making her way back to the table. "What about you?"

She looks around. "I am from right here. I grew up in this very house. That may be why I got my job here so easily."

I glance around the courtyard for the first time. I had been too hungry to care when we came outside. The courtyard itself was sitting right in the center of the building's U shape, with several people filling the picnic tables that fills the space.

Outside of the area we are in, there is a large building that looks like another garage over on the right. On the left is a giant ring. I can see a few people fighting from here. That must be the training area that Granny had told me about

There are a lot of people out here in general. "Are all these people out here shifters?" I ask them.

Adam nods. "Yes. No human is allowed to know about this place. To the outside world, we are just an extraordinarily rich family that lives here and nothing else."

"That's the reason for the gate and the guard house," Anna adds. "No one would know from the outside, but every single tower here, there are about fifty around the perimeter, has armed guards. There are patrols too."

Information is always good. Hopefully, it would be enough for whatever my grandparents were concerned about. "What does everyone change into?" I ask.

Anna spoke first. "Well, I am a hound shifter. A very small one. That is the reason I work here. All small animals get jobs in service, since we can't do much in a fight except bite someone on the ankles." I laugh along with the others.

It is interesting. I will find out how this world works. I'm not sure I am happy about some things. However, I will sit back and collect information for now.

Mack speaks for both her and her brother. "We are eyes in the sky," she said, but my confusion must have shown on my face because Adam adds, "Eagles, in our case, or any large bird, are eyes in the sky."

"Do you know anything?" Travis speaks up for the first time. He has a sneer on his face. "For being the leader's precious granddaughter, you would think you would at least know the basics of shifters."

"Oh, hell no!" I exclaim and stand. "What the hell is your problem with me? You don't even know me or anything about me."

He just rolls his eyes. "I know your type. You think you are so special, but let me tell you this. You can be your preppy high-class cheerleader self anywhere else, but you are nothing here."

His words hit me differently this time. The anger that always lives inside me slipped its leash. I step up to Travis, who had stands as I approach. Right in his face, I speak quietly, so only he could hear.

"You're going to regret this moment for the rest of your short life…"

My words are cut off because I could feel a fire burning deep within my gut that I have only felt twice in my life. I look to Anna with a wince of panic, and then I run as fast as I can. I have to get to the only place I know no one will know what is about to happen.

I shove my way into the conference room to find several people in the room. I know I don't have long; these people have to leave. Right this second. Not caring who any of them might be, I lock eyes with my grandmother with the same panic I showed Anna.

"Get out!" I said, but no one moves.

I recognize a few, including the couple I had met the night before, but not the others. They all look up, but no one is moving.

"I said, get the hell out!" I scream.

By this point, I was seconds from shedding my skin, and I have absolutely no idea what will happen if our secret is revealed. I guess it doesn't matter, because with a nod from my granny, everyone stands to leave. She lays her hands on my arms. "What happened, Cadence?"

I want to tell her. I want to stop this from happening, but I don't know how. It is as if the little stupid spat with Travis has shifted something inside me, and I can't put it back.

"Stop her," she tells the one remaining person in the room. "She needs to learn to control herself."

A man I hadn't even noticed walks over to me and snaps his fingers in my face. That alone causes the shift to speed up. I sink to the floor and curl in on myself, clutching my stomach that is currently on fire.

He is supposed to stop the shift, not make it come faster.

"Look at me, Cadence," he commands, but I am not paying attention. He notices. "Now, pay attention. You must calm down. Strong emotions can trigger an unwanted shift in new shifters. You must fight through it."

It wasn't his words that affected me; it was the door opening behind me.

Anna walks in, holding onto Travis. For someone so small, she has surprising strength, or he allowed her to drag him in. I think it is the latter.

"I am sorry, Madam Rose, but Travis here has something he wants to say." She shoves him toward me, not realizing that I am so close to actually spouting fur.

Somehow, just seeing them here, knowing that if I changed right here and now, the secret would be revealed, and all this careful planning would be over. Travis's life and maybe the finger snapper's would also be over. I wouldn't risk my family or Madi for them.

Travis steps forward with his head lowered. "I am sorry. I shouldn't have judged you like that, and I am sorry I upset you. I know better when it comes to new shifters." He looks down at the ground, but I am not sure he really means it.

My grandmother steps forward, frowning. "Someone needs to tell me what is going on here," she says, looking at everyone. "Mr. Carson, since it seems you caused my granddaughter's issue, you tell me."

He turns away from me to face Granny. I take deep breaths, trying to calm myself down. I have to calm down. I can not let them find out. I am better at this, or at least I should be. I have always been able to control my anger and turn it into something else. I would not fail because I refuse to allow it.

He tells her what happened out in the courtyard, basically, word for word. "Once Cadence ran inside, all my friends turned on me, demanding I come in here to apologize to her." That's why he was here. I knew he wasn't really sorry.

My grandmother is a real smart cookie because she saw it too. She didn't comment on it, though. She just nods.

"All right, now from this point forward, no one is to just come in here without permission," she looks to the little group by the door. That is where all the people I had just met outside is still standing. "You are dismissed."

They all say, "Yes, ma'am," at the same time, then turn and leave the room. Granny turns her attention back to me. "Now that you can speak, tell me what happened."

CHAPTER TEN

Cadence

I THROW MYSELF INTO the first chair. I think it was the one the guy had been sitting in, but I don't care.

"I don't know," I tell her the truth. I shake my head. "One minute, I was fine, sitting there chatting with the others. Travis had an attitude the entire time, sneering and rolling his eyes." I pause, trying to remember what the rage had felt like in that moment.

"As soon as he went off... it was like some secret fury I didn't even know existed came out, so much worse than my normal anger, and then the fire started. I didn't know what else to do, so I just ran here." I look at her, telling her without saying it that I was protecting the secret.

She smiles a small, knowing smile, letting me know she understands why I had come. She turns to the man still standing since I took his chair. "This here is Nathan Erickson. He's the trainer I was telling you about."

I glance at him but don't say anything. I am still mad that he had snapped his fingers in my face. He'd do well not to do that again. Next time I might just bite them off.

He just looks trashy to me, maybe because I don't like his attitude. He has that look that projects to the world he is better than anyone else.

"He has signed an agreement that anything he learns here is not to be shared with anyone. Enforceable by death." I am still going to be careful. I just don't trust him.

He finally joins us at the table. "Now, there is a certain way I like to do things, but the first thing we will do is go out and work on anger management. You will also shift..."

Granny interrupts him, reminding him to be discreet. He agrees, then stands and starts walking away.

"Come on, child,"

I growl. I am already in a bad mood. The way he had treated me before, that bad mood directed at him, and this only made it worse. He needs to cool his jets.

He leads the way to the little building I had seen behind the courtyard earlier. He opens the door to reveal the garage I had suspected it to be. It houses those little off-road vehicles. I have always wanted an ATV. He climbs into one and starts it up. The keys were left in the ignition. He just looks at the seat next to him like I was supposed to know exactly what he wanted.

With another growl, I climbed in.

"Anger problems," he mutters under his breath, but I hear him anyway. He hits a button on the roof, and the large door behind us opens. He backs out, then hits the button again, closing the door. He drives us to an open area at the back edge of the property, near the fence. The space has to be at least a mile from the house.

"Have you ever tried meditation for your anger management problems?" he asks. He gets off the ATV and leans against the fence, staring at me.

Oh, this man! He isn't bad looking if it weren't for his attitude. He is about my height, maybe an inch taller, with sky-blue eyes, my favorite color. His blonde hair is cropped military short. He seems hard, inside and out.

I shake my head. "No, I haven't because I don't have anger management problems." I pause. "Well, I didn't used to. I would get mad, but I would have no problem managing it, so it wasn't a problem."

He nods and sits on the ground. "Come sit down and let's get relaxed," he tells me, and does the same. I'm not sure how he expects me to relax knowing there is a stranger next to me. With everything else going on in my life, the last thing I want to do is relax.

"We are going to practice a little. Meditation is the key for most people. Once we have achieved relaxation, then we will practice bringing your beast in both directions."

I shrug and join him along the fence line. It takes a few minutes to get somewhat comfortable. I nod to him, ready as I could be.

"Okay, close your eyes." He pauses until I complied. "Now take a deep cleansing breath, slowly, in on three, out on three. Keep doing that." After a few breaths, he continues. "Now extend your counts to five. Good. Block everything out around you." This would be easier if I didn't hear his voice.

I obey, keeping my breathing steady. After a while, I feel my body relax. He waits until I am fully settled. "Now, Cadence, think of nothing except your beast."

I try to do that, but memories of my first shift confuse me and make me tense up, and I loose the sense of calm that I had finally achieved. I open my eyes to look at him. "Oops." I giggle.

"Try again," he snaps, but this time I ignore his attitude. After a few minutes of worrying about the mixed-up zoo, I find my calm again. A little quicker this time, once I have cleared my thoughts. "Just your beast this time, not the panic."

I try again, uncertain which animal to focus on. I picked one at random, the first I had seen. I picture the long black fur on one leg, flecked with white and gray. My body feels the same as it had then.

"Good!" he says. "Now send her back. Return to your breathing and relax." Sending the black fur back was easier now. Visualizing my normal body allows calm to return, and the burning sensation vanishes.

"Do it again. Bring your beast back." I obey, this time accidently focusing on the other leg with pure white fur. I heard him gasp, then snapped my focus back to the black leg. Apparently, he didn't noticed the shift.

"One more time," he says, but there is a catch to his voice; maybe he did notice. I think he is now seeing why he had to sign that agreement.

This time, when I brought the beast, I find myself focusing on the entire zoo. When the heat comes this time, I hear Nathan curse. I completely loose my grip, and my beast bursts free. The panther is making herself known. This time it didn't stop until I am completely animal, standing on four legs instead of two.

When I open my eyes, Nathan is gone. I look around and see him starting the ATV, fear etched across his face as he drives off, leaving me alone in a form no one could see.

Not knowing what else to do, I lay down and try to regain the earlier calm, but I couldn't. Unsure how long I have to remain in animal form, I try something else.

I lift my right paw up in front of my face and try to picture exactly what the other cat's colors were. After a few minutes, the blacks started to fade in places, leaving orange with black stripes. I almost giggled with excitement. I look at the stripes of black across my whole body and picture the small spots I thought I had seen right before I passed out. Sure enough, the stripes turn into little weird-shaped circles, like little rosettes. The color of my fur changed as well, turning from orange to a tawny color. My body itself changed a little too.

Okay, I can turn from one cat to the other, but could I turn from a cat to a dog? That would make it easier to hide my true form. I once again focused on the black fur that I had covering one leg. It took a while, but soon the burn returns, and the tawny and black fur changed, along with my body shape, to that of a complete dog. A huge dog, but still safer than anything else.

I look down at the scraps of clothing left. Nothing is salvageable. I should have brought my robe. Leaving the destroyed clothes behind, I run in the direction the ATV had gone.

Soon, the main house and courtyard comes into view. Since I have only used one door on each side, I know no other way in, so I head for the kitchen door.

When I reach it, I discover another problem: no hands. I couldn't open the door as a dog. That had been the whole point of running here in animal form. I could not shift back, but I saw a few people still at a nearby table.

I nudge the girl sitting on the bench and look at the door. After three tries, she just said no and turns away. The male across from her spoke clearly, "You are not allowed in the house in animal form. You will have to shift back."

I shake my head. Even if I was able, I would not shift here in front of everyone. I'm not entirely sure what would happen. I growl softly, then look back at the door.

When everyone at the table ignored me like I wasn't even there, I growl again, louder. This time I grab the sleeve of the rude girl with my teeth, trying to be careful, and drag her to the door. I am not trying to hurt her.

She squeaks but does as I want and opens the door. "Your funeral," she says with a shrug as she turns the handle.

As soon as it was open enough, I slip through and make my way back to the conference room. Since my granny is now using that as her office, I know that was where she will be.

When I get there, I have the same exact problem. This time, I place my paws on the wall and use my nose to press the intercom button. When no one answers, I press it repeatedly.

The door flies open. "What?!" My granny's power pushes at me, but I don't move. When she sees me, she steps back, letting me into the room. Nathan is sitting right there with my grandfather.

I run straight for him, knocking him onto the ground. I stand over him, looming in his face. My teeth snap so close to his nose I almost taste blood.

My grandfather rushes over but doesn't touch me. "Cadence, calm down, please. Don't hurt him."

I don't look up. I keep staring down Nathan. I growl again, though I only want to scare him. It works, so I back off and look at my grandpa.

"He left me." I try to tell him, but in human form, I don't think he can understand. *"He left me in the middle of my shift. I can't change back."*

His head snaps up. "He left you in what form?" He is not addressing the fact that he hears me, even though he is shocked.

I growl once again at Nathan, then turn back to Grandpa. *"Numeral Uno. The very one no one can see."* He just looks over my body; the body of the big black dog.

I know he is wondering how I would have been a dog if Nathan had left me in panther form. Before he could even ask, I picture the snow-white creature, and I feel my body move from one animal to the next. The more I do this, the easier it gets.

He opens his mouth as if he's going to speak and then closes it again. He tries a few more times before clearing his throat. "This will make things easier for keeping it a secret," he nods. More to himself than to me. "Yes. This is strange but good. Any time you shift, stay with the black dog."

The smart cookie that is my grandmother caught on quickly, even though she could only hear half of the conversation. "It will make it a lot easier if we can pass you off as the dog. I am unsure of the breed, but that doesn't matter."

"How...?" Nathan starts. "How are you both just taking this?" He has once again stood up. "I can't do this," he points at me. "She is the Black Dawn." He shakes his head over and over, muttering to himself. He turns to the door. "I will not be responsible if something happens to her. I'm sorry. I have to go."

My grandfather met him at the door. "Remember the agreement. If any harm comes to her because you said something..." he trails off, not finishing. We all know the punishment for breaking that agreement. Nathan just agrees and walks out the door. Seriously? What is his problem?

I looked down at myself. *"How do I change back?"* I asked them both. *"I'm stuck."*

They look at each other and turn back to me. "You should have to wait. That is normal until your body gets used to all the changes. The first few times, you must stay in one shape for at least a few hours. You should be able to change back later." It sounds like I am stuck in animal form for a while.

My grandfather looks at his watch and then back at me with a curious look on his face. "How many shapes do you have?" He pauses. "How did you know you could do that?"

While he starts to ask me questions, I see my granny going to the phone at the table. *"I'm not sure,"* I tell him. *"The first shift I remember differences in fur. The black of the dog, the white of the wolf. The three cats and one I thought I heard but haven't tried yet."* I tried to remember the sound that I heard right before I passed out, and I felt the burn of the shift.

Looking down at myself, I am definitely not a dog anymore. I am covered in brown fur. Standing up in my head comes close to hitting the ceiling. I have to be over eight feet tall. Inside the bear's body, I look down at my grandparents. *"Well, I guess that makes six."*

I sit on the floor right where I stood hard enough to make the table rattle. Fatigue is sweeping over my entire body, right as the burn of the shift started all on its own. Back in my human body, once again naked as the day I was born, I collapse on the ground. I have absolutely no energy left. For the third time in my life, my consciousness slipped away from me, and I pass out right there on the conference room floor.

Chapter Eleven

Hunter

T HE RINGING OF THE phone pulls me from a dream, well, a memory really. This was one of my favorite past lifetimes. It also happened to be the one I was able to spend the most time with my mate.

Fated mates are two souls that are fatefully bound together, the other half of your soul. The goddess gives us these mates and then puts us in each other's paths every single lifetime; it is up to us to finish the connection. We can choose not to love the same person again, but I'm not sure why we would. For me, it is my fated mate every time, even if that means I miss her in this lifetime and must wait until the next.

Several lifetimes ago, my mate and I decided to attempt to outrun fate. Just that thought alone makes me want to laugh and cry at the same time. What were we thinking? Neither would do us any good, in that lifetime or any other.

Sometimes, I wonder if we are not only destined to find each other in each new lifetime but to lose each other in everyone as well.

Sometimes I wonder if that is our only fate: death. That is all we ever seem to really do.

In each lifetime since the first, we have grown up and done what was needed to find one another. Once we did, it activated something that made death come for us every single damn time, making us lose each other once again.

In this memory dream, Lizzy and I had found each other young. We were only about ten years old when my family moved next door to hers. At the time, we did not know who we were to each other; we just knew we had an instant connection. I had been glorious, being able to spend so much time with my best friend.

We had eight long years to be together during that lifetime. Eight glorious years to grow up, to get to know each other all over again, to fall in love. We were each other's everything. We spent every waking hour of those eight years together.

When we shifted for the first time and our memories started coming back, hers were a little faster than mine. That is the way it always was. This time, we decided we would fight the bitch called fate. Fuck her. However, it did not happen as we planned.

We packed only what we could carry on our backs, and we ran. The witches already knew we were here, so our only choice was to run. We had seen the witches hovering, watching our every move. I am surprised she didn't come for us sooner.

On our third night, we found a little cabin nestled in a clearing at the foot of some mountains. The views were amazing, but we were after safety. A warm bed to sleep in. It was not much, just a one-room place away from the cold. There was a little creek not far away and a wood stove. We were together, so we were happy.

For a few short hours, the cabin was everything we wanted in life. Lizzy started a stew on the wood stove while I went to grab some more firewood. We would eat, sleep, make love, and be gone by daylight. That was our plan. Keep moving so that we could stay a step ahead of Felicia and her death wish.

When I dropped the firewood off at the cabin, I found it empty. At first, I started to wonder if Felicia had already been there until I saw that the water bucket was missing as well. I went to find my love. I found her at the creek.

She had the missing water bucket sitting beside her while she stared out at the beautiful landscape that surrounded the little clearing. Her long black hair cascaded down her back with a beautiful shine caused by the fading light. I knew that if she turned around, her bright green eyes that always seemed to sparkle would find me instantly, lighting up her stunning features from within.

Not able to stand and watch my beloved any longer, I came up behind her, wrapped my arms around her waist, and rested my head on her shoulder. "Hello, love." I greeted her the simple way I had been doing for countless lifetimes.

After a moment of just soaking her warmth deep into my soul, I leaned down and placed a small kiss on her lips and then took her hand to lead her back to the cabin. She needed to warm her chilled skin, and I would not be the one to cause her any discomfort.

We only made it about halfway back to the cabin before the bitch named fate found us in the form of about thirty or so witches. I didn't take the time to count them.

They came out of the trees in a way that suggested a planned attack. They surrounded us within seconds, cutting off any chance at escape. The chant they spoke swelled in volume, causing a sluggish feeling, but it was not anything we couldn't handle.

I locked eyes with Lizzie, and she nodded. That was all it took. We instantly shed our human skin, ignoring the burn. There is no time for the pain, just action.

I gave a last goodbye to the love of my lifetimes. I knew, I'm sure she did as well, that this was the end again. We would meet again in the next lifetime before turning to face the witches on my side. We may be going down today, but we will take at least a few of them with us.

The phone on the bedside table vibrates again, alerting me to a voicemail, pulling me out of my memories. It reminds me of what woke me in the first place. Glancing over at the offending device, I sigh.

I pick it up to see a missed call with a voicemail from the Central Region again. She must be getting desperate. I can only imagine why. There are not many of us trainers, nowhere near as many as we need. I listen to the voicemail as I sit up. There will be no going back to sleep now.

Sighing again, I get up to pack the little I have here. I will give in this time and forego my vacation, but I will not stay for the normal time. Just long enough for the new shifter to get a basic understanding. They can figure it out from there. I return the call after I have placed all my belongings into the car. I will be on the next flight out.

Chapter Twelve

Cadence

D REAMS ARE WEIRD; VIVID dreams are worse. One second, you are lying unconscious on your grandparents' conference room floor, and the next, you are being thrust through time. I blink to clear my dream vision. I know I am dreaming because I have never been in this little cabin before.

Dream me was cooking on an old wood stove. Not the fancy ones either. These were the heavy-built, cast-iron ones that had a flat top that you could place pots on. The main use of them was to heat small spaces.

In one hand, I held a wooden spoon that I was currently using to stir the contents of the pot; in the other, I held the lid. Stirring revealed some sort of stock, with a few vegetables floating within. The left hand held the lid, which I placed on the pot after I stirred it.

Setting the spoon down, I walked over to the corner of the room to pick up a bucket. The bucket was metal, and I knew that it was used for carrying water. Seeing that it was currently empty, I headed to the door.

There wasn't much in the room itself. A bed sat in the corner near the heater, but not close enough for it to catch fire. There were two chairs and a water basin that would be used to clean up.

It didn't matter what was in the little cabin, though. We would not be here long. They were planning to leave again in the morning. They knew they could not sit long, but it was nice to get a little break from all the running. To have just a little downtime to be with each other.

Taking the water bucket with me out of the door, I looked around. I was looking for someone but wasn't sure who it was. I stood in front of the little cabin for a moment to take in the surreal surroundings. The cabin itself was sitting in a small clearing, small enough that it held only the cabin. There was access to a creek. That is where I am headed.

I made my way to the creek without a care in the world. I knew we would be safe for the moment. I should care about many things, but I would not let my worries bother me tonight. We would face all those things in the morning, like we always do. As a team. For now, I would collect this water and finish cooking the hot meal I was currently working on; who knew when we would get another?

After filling my bucket, I stand and close my eyes, just taking a deep breath of the fresh mountain air. As I stood there, I felt a pair of strong arms wrap around my waist from behind. I wasn't scared, though, even though we were hunted. I could never fear the person these arms belonged to.

I look over my shoulder as I turn to face him, the bucket forgotten on the ground beside me. I smile into the face of my beloved. I run my hands up his arms to wrap my arms around his neck before standing on the tips of my toes to give him a small kiss right on his chin. My fingers run up into his short brown hair. He had to cut it recently, and I was already missing the longer locks. The most beautiful set of cerulean blue eyes hiding behind thick and full lashes that match his hair stare back at me. This has always been my favorite color, and until this moment, I didn't know why.

"Hello, love." He greets me in that deep voice of his that does funny things to my insides. I will never get used to the reaction that I get just from hearing his voice. He leans down to kiss me before releasing his hold on my waist. He takes possession of my hand and starts to pull me away from the breathtaking view of the creek and the mountains beyond. I stopped him long enough to grab my bucket.

He was heading in the direction of the little cabin. I needed to get back before my food was burnt anyway. I follow him, but we never make it back. About halfway there, we saw a group appear from the trees off to the right.

They were just starting to enter the clearing; there had to be over thirty people. They formed a half-circle right outside the trees and started chanting. It felt as if they were trying to hold us, but whatever they were doing only slowed us down. It was like walking in sand, but we were still able to move. It was just enough to get them into position, surrounding us.

The man and I shifted at the same time, breaking the spell that they had cast on us. His tiger form appeared almost instantly—the most beautiful tiger I have ever seen. I was a lot darker than a normal tiger, almost as if it was mixed with something darker. Instead of the normal orange and black stripes you see on most, his was a dark gray that held a hint of orange, with the classic grey stripes. His beautiful blue eyes were the same color in animal form.

I had no idea who these people were, other than the fact that they were witches. All I knew was that we were greatly outnumbered. We backed up into each other, intertwining our tails for a moment, then faced off with our enemies.

"Cadence!" I hear someone scream my name. The use of my real name in the here and now pulls me from the vivid dream. It is good timing, too, because I was about to die. I know I was. I could feel it deep within my bones.

Opening my eyes, I find myself in my bed at the Farm. The canopy above me is swaying as if it had been cut. Anna is standing at the foot of the bed, staring at me. There are little bits of something that looks like little white feathers in the air all around us. Anna's hands are covering her gaping mouth. I try to sit up to see what is happening, but my body doesn't respond.

I look down at my body to see if there is any damage from the witches that had attacked us, only to find my body covered in fur—the fur of my panther. My eyes rise to find that Anna has not moved.

Crap... the cat is out of the bag.

I take a few breaths to try to calm myself, but after the adrenaline rush caused by the dream and being woken by my friend, I can't bring on the shift. Again. There is no way I will be finding any calm anytime soon.

I look back at Anna. "*Close your mouth,*" I giggle as I tell her. "*I guess my secret is out, but you cannot under any circumstances tell anyone.*"

I roll over and settle again.

I would not lie here, especially after that dream with my soft underbelly exposed. Not to mention my lady parts. Even if they are in animal form at the moment. Neither my cat nor my dignity will allow it.

"You...you..." she stutters. "You are the...Black Dawn?" It really wasn't a question. It just came out higher than expected. I nod. I need to try to make this easier. I picture the black dog and will myself to change. Even if I can not retake human form, I can change animals.

"How?" she starts again, this time speaking clearly. She tilts her head slightly. "Did you talk to me before?"

I nod again. "*I can speak in my beast form.*" I tilt my head sideways, thinking, mirroring her action. It must be the dog in us. "*Well, I can speak in any form. Apparently, there are a few differences. I am not like normal shifters. I was serious; it is imperative that you not tell a soul what you have seen here today.*"

She then starts firing questions without even giving me a chance to answer, but that is to be expected. Just sitting here talking is starting to calm the adrenaline rush from earlier. I am still not able to shift back, though.

"Who all knows about you?" was her last question. So, I focus on that one alone for now.

"*My grandparents and my parents were with me when I shifted. The beta couple was told once we arrived. Then that little snot, Nathan. I do not like him. Do you know he left me, in animal form, on my second shift? I was stuck and didn't even know how to change back.*"

Her mouth drops open. "No way. That's bull. He should have known better." She shakes her head. "It's good that no one else knows. Especially with you being so new to the shifter world. How is that anyway?"

I could understand the question. "*My dad is apparently a carrier but doesn't shift. My mother is human. They never expected me to shift in the first place, so there was no reason for me to live any differently than a human. Until I shifted into something even they couldn't predict. The odds were definitely stacked against me. It was a shock to everyone there that I not only shifted, but shifted into... the whole freaking zoo.*"

She just stares at me for a moment. "What do you mean? Is there more than the panther and the Newfoundland mix?" I am guessing that that was the breed of the dog I was currently sitting in. I have heard of them but never seen one before.

I give her the truth. I am just going to have to trust her. No going back now. "*I have three cats: panther, tiger, and leopard. There is the dog, the wolf, and the* bear." I hoped that was all. "*Oh... I almost forgot the wing. I may be able to change into a large bird. I haven't tried that one yet,* though."

She was quiet for a moment. "What you need is a little shifter one-oh-one." She then sits on the bench at the end of the bed. She pulls her legs under her and gets comfortable. I just nod at her because I agree. If I am to survive in this world, I need information.

"The summit meeting starts in a few hours. That was the original reason for coming in here. We need you, human though. No animal forms allowed in the house."

As she talked, I took stock of my surroundings. I was in my room, in my bed, in dog form, but it would need to be replaced. The floating feathers I had been seeing this entire time were, in fact, parts of the bed. I had apparently shifted and destroyed the bed. There is a spring poking into my butt. I shift slightly to get the spring out of my rear end, then look back to Anna as she starts speaking again.

She settles down on the end of my bed, on a part that was not damaged. "Alright, let's start with the basics." She shifts to get comfortable, then looks back at me. "There are several types of shifters. If you can think of the animal, there is probably a shifter version of that same animal. Within the shifter community as a whole, there are classes. Each class means something different." She pauses.

"For example, the smaller animals are the servants," she sneers. She didn't like this fact. "The larger ones, like some large birds, are scouts and are often referred to as 'Eyes in the Sky.' Large dogs are used for 'Search and Rescue,' sometimes tracking. It all depends on the breed. The larger animals, like cats, wolves, bears, buffalo, bison, etc., are our warriors."

She then goes on to tell me about the rules. "Some are basic, like you cannot reveal yourself to a human. No harming humans. It is our job to protect the humans after all."

Once I was able to change into my human form, I did so. Each shift came faster and without as much pain. Hopefully, one day soon, I will get a better handle on all this stuff.

After I shower off the sweat from the dream, I dress in another basic T-shirt and jeans. I have to remember to cover the birthmark that has somehow darkened even more. It is starting to look more like a tattoo instead of what it actually is.

I rejoin Anna in my bedroom, then we make our way to the kitchen. I have just enough time to grab some food, then have to go find my grandparents.

With food in tow, we make our way to the same table as before. Mack, Adam, and Travis are already sitting there. "Hey, guys," I say to the twins. I still do not trust Travis, and I probably never will.

They all say hi, then we started to eat. "Hey…" Adam starts. "Do you like to swim? Or do you like going to the beach?"

I nod. "I love to swim. My best friend back home has a pool party every year."

"We are going into town tomorrow for some lunch and some beach time. My best friend is coming into town, and we want to hang out before he starts his new job," he informs me. "Want to go?"

I think about it. I have not left the Farm once since I got here. It would also give me some more time to get to know the people I would be spending the next three months with. "Yes," I tell him, "I will have to check with Granny before then." I have responsibilities and secrets to keep. I couldn't just run off whenever I wanted to, unfortunately.

Chapter Thirteen

Cadence

WE TALK A BIT about different things that we like and dislike. Travis even joined in on the conversation like a real boy. I laugh to myself. I don't have much time right now, but maybe I could talk to them more on the beach trip. Right now, I have to go.

I have to attend the Summit meeting. Apparently, this meeting happens every three months. Each leader and two representatives will be attending from each region. I am undercover, taking the place of the female beta. She didn't like it, but since she knows who and what I am, she accepts it.

It had been drilled into me to play a part. I was to walk in, stand next to the beta male, and keep my mouth shut at all times. No matter what was said, I wasn't allowed to talk. We are holding our cards close to our chest.

I gather my dishes and return them to the kitchen before making my way back to the conference room.

I follow my instructions perfectly. I walk in, look around to find the beta, and when I spot him against the wall behind my grandparents, I make my way over to him, leaning against the wall right beside him. I guess I am the last person to arrive. Oops, my bad.

I look around the room. At the table, there are six clear sections of people. One person per section, except my grandparents. Each person at the table has two people standing behind them. These are the area leaders and their diplomats.

My grandfather stands up and clears his throat, calling the meeting to attention. Apparently, everybody is here. "Welcome to the Central Region. We want to thank you all for coming." He looks around the room. "I see a few unfamiliar faces, so I want to take a moment to go around the table for introductions. Please take a moment to introduce yourself and tell us who your diplomats are." He pauss to look down at Granny.

"I am Robert Robinson, and this is my wife, Rose. We are the leaders of the Central Region. Most of you know my beta, but the young lady standing next to him is our granddaughter, Cadence Robinson." He nods to the man on his right, then sits back down.

The man stands up, straightening his suit. He has dark hair and dark skin. I could already tell he is from a place that has lots of sunshine. You could see it in the fine lines around his eyes. He isn't incredibly old, maybe mid-thirties.

"Hello everyone," he starts with a smile. "I am Carlos Rodriguez. I am the leader of the Southern Region. The people behind me." He motions to the pair behind him. The two men standing behind him looks like younger versions of himself. They have to be twins. "These are my sons, Anakoni and Kai." He sits back down.

The next man stands up. He has a sneer on his face as he looks around the room. This man has jet black hair that is slicked over to the side. He looks exactly like a slimy mob boss. "This is completely unnecessary," he spat. "Since the important ones sitting at this table already know one another..." He looks right at me with a look of disgust on his face. "Just because your half-breed mutt is here, you want everyone to do this shit." He sits back down without saying more.

Not knowing if I could send messages while in human form to another in human form, I look at my grandfather and try. If I didn't try, I'd never know. "*That must be the New York leader you were warning me about.*" His head jerks up, and his eyes lock with mine. I almost laugh. It worked. He nods, looking back to the Eastern leader.

"Fine. I will do it since I am hosting this quarter." He smiles at the Eastern leader, knowing it is just pissing him off. "Anthony Rogers, AKA Tony, from the Eastern Region and his diplomats." He points behind Tony.

The sight of the two behind the eastern leader makes my jaw drop. The male and female standing behind Anthony are the two rude ones from yesterday. They had refused to open the door. "Jessica Reynolds and Tony Junior," my grandfather says. I guess I had threatened and even dragged the diplomats from the Eastern area. That is why senior was so mad.

Jessica was standing there with the same look her father had. She is rubbing her arm, right where I had grabbed her. Her sleeve slides up slightly, revealing a white bandage on her already pale skin. The younger Tony has a smile on his face, like he finds this all funny.

Senior is still looking at me. "I see you recognize them." I shrug. He turns back to my grandparents. "Why is she even here? She is nothing, just a mongrel. There is no room here for trash like her."

My grandmother looks to me with a knowing look, then addresses the Eastern leader. "First of all, I would recommend that you not speak about my granddaughter this way in my own territory. With it being my territory, you have no say in who we choose to have as our delegates. Now sit down and shut up, so we can finish this." He does as he is told, but you could see he is not happy.

The next in line stands. This man, however, is the opposite of the Eastern leader. Pale skin and even paler hair. His clear ice-blue eyes lock onto me. He addresses me with a smile. "I am Franklin. I am the leader of the Northern Region, and these lovely people behind me are my beta pair." He turns to smile at the two females behind him.

Both stand proud. The one on the left has blonde hair and blue eyes, and the one on the right reminds me a lot of Mack; she has the same caramel-colored skin. "Greta and Sophia," Franklin says as he takes his seat once again, never losing his smile.

The next in line is a bombshell of a woman. Everything about her is beautiful. She screams supermodel never even saying a word. She has long dark hair flowing down her back. She has the prettiest grass green eyes I have ever seen. "Hello all. I am Sarah McClain. I am the West Coast Region leader." she looks behind her to assure her betas are still there. "My beta couple. Eric and Jonathan." she sits back down.

The next one was a heaver set woman with deep brown hair. "Elena Love, at your service. Natasha and Robbie are behind me." She never even stood. She also didn't mention where she was from. I would remember to ask again later.

"Now let's get down to business," my grandfather tells everyone.

For the next several minutes, each region takes turns talking about the happenings in their regions. It looked like there is a set order to things and they are following a script. Since this meeting happens so often, this is probably how they did it each time.

In almost every region, there are several missing shifters. Some has even been found dead. This is concerning and I know almost nothing about this world. If I am feeling this way, I could only imagine how the leaders of each region, other than Easterners, are feeling with dead and missing friends.

As the meeting is wrapping up, my grandmother addresses the room. "Has anyone seen anything that could be the Black Dawn? We figured they would come forward by now," she asks as we had planned.

We had planned it this way so that we would appear to be just as curious as everyone else to gather information on our new leader. This is just a way to hold my identity a little longer, so the people in this room would not know that she is standing right in front of them this entire time. As the half-breed as one called me.

It opens discussions about me, but we are all shocked when the Eastern leader is the one to speak up. "I believe I have a line on him." Sexist pig. "We believe he is in upstate New York." Everyone nods like this is a possibility.

"*Since when can I teleport?*" I ask my grandmother, also sending her the impression of me changing into a male. She almost laughs but covers it with a cough, grabbing the glass of water in front of her to take a sip. "Good, Tony. Please keep us informed. I would love to meet *him*," she says to him, putting emphasis on the last word.

What I really want to do was grab hold of my natural C cup breasts and ask him when I became a man. I wouldn't though, because that would be telling him exactly who I am and what we are hiding.

I wonder what the Eastern Region leader would gain from this lie. Lying about the Black Dawn couldn't give them more than attention. And if he really is in the mob, you would think he wouldn't want the attention. Unless there is some other unknown reason, it served no purpose. He still doesn't have to be a sexist pig.

After an ungodly amount of time talking about random boring shifter stuff, the meeting finally ended. I am so ready to sit down. All the Region leaders and their delegates are finally leaving. Thank the goddess. As they all leave, Emily, the female beta, comes in, closing the door behind her, once again making the room soundproof.

"That was interesting," Jameson says, then filled Emily in on the details of the meeting. "I'm not sure what he gains from these lies," he adds, mirroring my thoughts from earlier. No one has anything else to add, and no one knows why.

CHAPTER FOURTEEN

Cadence

As soon as I have the chance, I bring up the day trip to the beach. "Do we have anything planned for tomorrow?"

My grandmother shakes her head. "Not as of now. The replacement trainer will not be here until tomorrow evening, so you have the morning free. He is flying in from Alaska."

"Anna introduced me to some of her friends, as you know from earlier. Adam has a friend coming into town tomorrow. Everyone is going to spend the day in Galveston with the twins' friend. I have been invited. I want to go."

She doesn't respond for a moment. "I am sorry, but you really shouldn't take the risk. I would prefer it if you were safe here at the Farm. We can keep you alive."

"Is there anything we can do? I really want to go. I just can't stay here locked up like a prisoner forever." That's what it feels like when she tells me that I can't leave. I cannot go from the life I had in Missouri to being locked up on this massive property for three months. I would go insane.

They agree with that, but we still need to be safe. If whoever it was that is after me caught me out alone or even surrounded by the few friends, I have to think about more than my own feelings, because if they are correct, then it could be disastrous.

"I have an idea," Emily starts. She then looks to her husband, who happened to be the beta male, with a secret smile. "We could go with them," she says to her husband.

After a beat, Jameson agrees. "Yes, we can go with them. That would allow Cadence to go have a little fun with her friends. With us there, she would be safer," he pauses. "That's eight shifters, including the Black Dawn herself." He looks to my grandmother to see if she agrees.

My grandmother finally agreed. I leave them to talk over the details of how they would keep me safe and then go to find Anna. I locate her in her room, which happens to be next to mine. That is how she had heard me earlier.

Twenty minutes later, I am back in my room. I flopped down on my bed and pull out the shiny new phone that I got for my birthday. Even though I have met a few people here, I am lonely. I miss my family. I miss my best friend. So much it hurt.

I dial Madi's home number first. She doesn't have a mobile yet. After three rings, I hear the voice I have been waiting to hear. "Hello."

"Hey Madi," I mutter knowing I am in trouble.

"Hey girl. Your mom told me you left the state, and you didn't even call me!" She sounds not only hurt but mad, and I couldn't blame her. I would feel the same way if the roles were reversed.

"I know," I sigh loudly. "I didn't have much time, and it was so early." I have to figure out something to tell her that does not reveal the real reason that I had to leave. "I can't believe they forced me to leave like that."

We stay on the phone longer than we should have, but I would not go without talking to her. Thinking back now, I wonder if this is the reason they bought me this phone for my birthday. If they knew that if I shifted, I would have to pack up and move. If they wanted me to have a way to keep in contact if that happened.

I didn't want to be here. I want to be at home with my parents and my friends. But I made a promise. I would do my three months, and then I would be with them again. Although I am super excited about getting out tomorrow, I have never been on a ferry and I have only been to a beach once.

As soon as I fell asleep, I find myself once again locked in a vivid dream. I sure hope it is a dream anyway. I didn't recognize my surroundings once again.

I was a child this time. I couldn't be much older than five or six years old. I knew it was me, or it felt that way. I was walking down the beach at the water's edge. I could smell the fishy odor that came from the one trip we had taken to the ocean, so it must be salt water.

There was a woman on my right, my mother. She had blonde hair that fell around her shoulders in pretty waves. My father was on my left, holding my hand as well. He had dark hair and bright eyes. We were all wearing our swimsuits because we had been swimming in the water not far from where we were now.

Every few steps, my parents would stop and swing my small body by my arms, and I would giggle so loudly. As soon as my feet hit the hot sand, I would start begging for them to do it again.

The beach was deserted. It looked as if it may have even been a secluded area. As we made it back to the chairs and my sandcastle, my father went back to the house to get us all drinks. Swimming was thirsty work, but we weren't allowed to drink the ocean water.

Once my father was out of sight, three new people walked up to where my mother and I sat waiting for my father to return.

There was one woman and two men. The woman stepped up to my mother, and the men acted as if they were going to keep walking, only to circle up behind us to cage us in.

My mother grabbed hold of my arm, accidentally hurting the spot where she held on. I watched as a woman stopped right in front of us. There was something wrong with Mommy, but I didn't know what it was.

The woman started talking to my mother at first, but I couldn't understand what was being said. Then I understood completely. The woman asked again about the Kitty birthmark that is on my back. There was something special about it.

While the lady had my mother distracted, the man had been moving closer. The bigger one reached out and pulled me into his arms, breaking the tight hold my mother had on my other arm. He pulled so hard that I heard a noise come from my shoulder. It hurt so badly I cried out in pain.

As soon as the man had his hands on me, the lady pulled a knife and shoved it into my mother's stomach. My cries of pain changed to heart-wrenching screams, but the sound was cut off by the man's hand coming up to cover my mouth.

The woman pulls the knife from my mother's stomach, laughing. She walked over to me. I struggled in the man's grip. I wanted loose. This woman was going to hurt me. I could see it in her eyes.

Right then, my father came running out of the house. The woman just laughed again. "He will never make it in time," the woman started chanting then, the world around me went dark.

I wake with a gasp. I am back in my own bed at the Farm. But my mind is still there with that woman who had just killed my mother. I am dripping with sweat. The bed is soaking wet. I am, however, still human. That is a bonus. I look over at the clock on the bedside table. It is already after five o'clock in the morning. There is no chance of any more sleep.

So, I climb out of bed and go straight to the bathroom to wash all the sweat off my body. I have a long, fun day ahead of me, and I wasn't going to let these dreams put a damper on that.

Once I was clean and calmed down again, I dress in a pair of jean shorts and a tank top. Slipping into my flip flops, I make my way to Anna's room.

I keep thinking over the dream. It seems to me that if that had in fact been a memory that I had been killed just for having that birthmark. I pat the back of my shoulders to assure myself that it was covered completely. I never want to go through that again.

I mentally shake myself to clear the images of blood and death. I knock on the door in front of me quietly. I don't want to wake anyone else up down the hall. Anna opens the door and is fully dressed. Just like I expected her to be. For once, she wasn't wearing the blue on blue of her work uniform.

We both stand there checking each other out. She has on a bright pink tank top. The strings of her bikini are sticking out at the top. From the waist down, she matches me. Jean shorts and flip flops.

She steps back so that I can enter her room. Her space looks a lot like mine. Same basic furniture, same color on the walls, but hers is a lot smaller. It looks like she doesn't have an attached bathroom. She must use the one right up the hall. It makes me wonder how many people share the one bathroom.

I sit down on the foot of her bed. "When do we leave?" I am so ready to get out of here. Even if it is just for a little while. I can still feel a little of the effects from the dream. She just chuckles at me. She doesn't realize how stir-crazy I am. The funny thing is, I was fine until it was mentioned that there was a possibility of leaving.

She sits down on the other side of the bed. "We are going to meet up with the others at breakfast, then head out as soon as we find the beta pair." She shakes her head. "I still don't see why they are being forced to go. We don't need adult supervision when we are adults now."

I shrug. "After my dream last night, I would welcome some extra protection." Before she could even ask, I tell her about the dream from the night before and the one before that, too.

I need to ask someone. Anna happens to be one of the few people who knew about me, so, I am hoping that she will know what is going on. If nothing else, I could use her as a sounding board.

"It sounds to me like your memories are coming in. You are starting to remember your past lives—some of them at least." She pauses. "Well, how you died in them."

She then went on to explain a little more about the memories. "With shifters, we are able to assess most of our past lives. The memories start to come in slowly after we shift for the first time." She hesitates. "Some shifters are able to get all of their past life memories; some only get some. This takes time, though. Normally, about six months or so for the lucky ones. I am still getting mine in bits and pieces, just like you are."

"Great, so I have to deal with these dreams for that long." I sigh and flop back on her bed.

"Not necessary. With you being the Black Dawn, who knows what will happen?" She went on to explain a bit more. "For normal shifters, it takes a while. That is the most frustrating thing. Ugh, I hate it. Just give them all to me at once. But then again, it may be an overload of information."

By the time she is finished explaining all she knows about the memories, it was time to go meet up with the others.

On our way down the stairs, the beta couple found us, saving us the trouble of having to search for them after we finish eating.

"Good morning," Emily greets us. "Rose asked me to give you this." She hands me some cash. I didn't even grab my wallet from my room, so I am glad she thought of money. "She also asked me to tell you to be safe but have fun." She smiles.

I thank her as I stuffed the money into the back pocket of my shorts.

My cellphone, I didn't forget. It is in the other pocket. After agreeing to a meet-up time with the betas after breakfast, we make our way down the hall to the dining room.

As soon as we enter, we are assaulted by the smell of bacon. Bacon is not the only thing on the menu for today. There are pancakes and waffles, their sweetness filling the air along with the smell of the bacon.

There are several types of eggs: scrambled, fried, even boiled. Along with the normal fixings that you could get any other time of the day.

I already know it will not be like my mother's cooking, but it is a close second. I load my plate with bacon and scrambled eggs before grabbing toast and a water bottle. I wait for Anna, then we make our way to the table with our friends.

After the greetings are over, we all sit and ate our food, mostly in silence. Once we are finished and the plates are cleared away, Adam gets our attention.

"So, we still have a few minutes before the meet-up time, so I guess now is a good time to fill you in on what the plan for the day is." He pauses. "The first thing we will do is go down to Galveston and take the ferry across the water. The ferry is great if you have never been on one."

I shake my head at him, letting him know that I have not. "A ferry is a giant boat that you can drive your car onto, along with a bunch of other people, and then you can get out of your car and walk around. If you watch closely, you can even see the dolphins jump right out of the water following the boat."

That sounds exciting. I am getting so hyped up about this trip, I am bouncing in my seat. Living in Missouri doesn't give you the chance to do exciting stuff like this. I guess that's one good thing about my trip away from home. Otherwise, I would probably never leave Missouri.

Adam has finished talking about the ferry and is moving on. "Once we drive off the ferry, we will be going like ten minutes up the road to a smaller beach. It's not excessively big, but there are also not a lot of people who use that beach."

I like the sound of that. "Hunter, my friend, will be meeting us there at the beach." I wonder for a moment if it was the same Hunter who is coming to train me tonight.

When the time comes to meet out front, we all go in a group to find the betas already have two cars ready to go. After some discussion, all the girls pile into one car and the boys in the other.

Once we are on the road, following the boys' car, Mack turns to Anna and me. "I am so excited." She starts bouncing in her seat, as much as the seat belt will allow. "I have not seen Hunter in ages." She starts to fan herself.

Anna and I exchange a look. After all the time spent with her, and the fact that she knows my secret, I feel a little closer to her. "I am guessing you like Hunter?" I ask Mack.

"Who wouldn't? He is H.O.T.!" She giggles to herself.

"Why are you not dating him then?" Anna asks.

I just sit there and wait for her answer. There is something deep down inside of me that does not like the fact that she likes him like that. I have no clue why though because I have never even met this person. Why the green-eyed monster is on my shoulders, I wish I knew. It is the strangest reaction.

Mack loses some of her shine. "I wish." She turns thoughtful. "I tried more than once. Believe me, I have tried, but he refuses. He says there is only one girl for him, and he will not even date anyone else."

Emily glances at Mack in the rearview mirror. She doesn't say anything, but it looks like she wants to.

I do not say anything either. I don't know much about relationships. I have never been in one. Never wanted to be in one. At one time, I thought I might be defective, but now it does not bother me as much. So, what? I don't like boys. I don't like girls either.

"I see," Anna says, bringing me out of my head and back to the conversation.

"What about you guys?" Mack looks at me. "I know you just got here, but did you break any hearts when you left home?"

I shake my head. "The only hearts I broke were my best friend's and my mother's." I laugh.

Anna wags her eyebrows. "So, is she more than just a friend?"

I gag. "Ew, no!" Anna's face drops. I think she may have taken that the wrong way. "Not like that. She is just my best friend, no extras. She may like girls. There is no problem with that part, but I couldn't ever be with her like that. She is more like a sister." I think I just learned something important about my new friend.

We talk and laugh about any and everything over the next hour. It takes that long to get to the ferry. We pull up behind the boys' car, but there is no ferry in sight. It looks like we will be here for a while.

CHAPTER FIFTEEN

Cadence

I T SEEMS LIKE WE have to wait forever, moving a few feet at a time before it was finally our turn to drive on the massive vessel. I am sure glad it is not me driving this car and trying to park so close to the other vehicles.

Once it is safe to get out, we did. Adam wants to show me everything there was to see since this was my first time on a ferry. Heck, it is the first time I have ever been on a boat. So, everything was new and shiny. We did, in fact, get to see a few dolphins break the surface of the water.

When it is time to get back into the cars, I sigh. I am not ready for our ride to be over. This time, we did the same as last time; all the guys ride in one car and the girls in the other. We were all going to the same place, and we each have a beta to keep us safe.

We drive for another twenty minutes and several turns. Half of that is spent just getting off the boat. At the last turn, the boys' car and ours are separated by a car that is too slow to take off, and us girls get stuck at the traffic light. Mack ends up having to showing us which way to go because Emily has not even been to this beach before.

Mack leads us to a parking area. We can see the sandy beach from where we park. Adam, Travis, and Jameson are standing next to a man who is still sitting on a motorcycle. We end up having to park a few rows back as there isn't any space closer. As soon as the car is in park, Mack jumps out of the car and runs to meet up with the guys.

The rest of us make our way a lot slower. There is no reason for us to run. We don't even know this person that we are meeting, but Mack is still friends with him even though he has turned her down. I get the feeling that she is still a little in love with him and hopes he will change his mind.

As we approach the group, I hear the man speak for the first time. "Since when does the beta get sent with a bunch of teens going to the beach? Is there something going on that I don't know about?"

Somehow, that voice sounded familiar. I cannot for the life of me place where I have heard it, but I know I have. Now the tone is off a little bit, but it is the same voice.

Adam chuckles. "No... this is the first time that has happened." He tells him, then looks over to where we are coming up behind where the man is now standing. "It's probably because their granddaughter is with us." He says it all in a neutral tone, but I wonder if he would rather I go back.

I don't beat around the bush about it. "I can always leave," I tell him. "The betas and I can just go back to the Farm if it's that much trouble." I start to turn around to Emily, who is standing right next to me, but the sound of my voice must have caught Hunter's attention.

He turns just enough for me to see a beautiful set of familiar cerulean-blue eyes and long tasseled brown hair that almost touches his brow. I just stand there and stare. He is doing the exact same thing. I have seen that handsome face before. It seems so familiar yet just a stranger.

The man standing before me, in slick black leather chaps, which cover a nice ass in blue jeans, is the very man of my dreams. In fact, my dream just two nights ago. We had been a couple in that dream. I could feel the love and connection even though it was all happening inside one very vivid dream.

Mack was correct about the hotness of her friend.

I guess we have stood there in silence long enough for everyone to start looking between us. "Do you two know each other?" Mack asks with a hint of disappointment in her voice. After her advances had been turned down, I could only imagine how she felt. Just the way he is looking at me would hurt, at least a little.

Hunter pulls his attention away from me, at last breaking the trance I had been in. For a few moments, I had been feeling everything I had experienced in the dream. When the reality was, I have never met this man. "Not in this lifetime," he answers her question, mirroring my thoughts.

"Is she the one you were telling me about?" Mack asks Hunter. There's a mix of disappointment from before and a little excitement, too. She really is happy for him. He just nods and turns back to look at me once more.

Adam steps forward. "Hunter Riggs, this is Cadence Robinson. Granddaughter of Rose and Robert and the reason the betas are here." He looks at me, "and no, I don't want you to leave. You are stuck with us now."

Hunter is still looking at me. There is a bit of longing on his face. "Do you have your memories?" He asks softly, "Do you know who I am?"

I think about how to answer. I do not really want to say much while we have an audience. Anna is the only one here who knows about the dreams. "No..." I say, but add in a whisper, "... and yes."

He must have heard me because he nods. "Then we start from the beginning," he smiles. I had never seen such a sexy smile before. "That's the fun way," he says, looking around at everyone else. "Who's ready to go to the beach?"

Hunter waits for me to reach his side. "Did you bring a swimsuit?" He looks to where the other girls are. They are already shedding clothes to get to the bikinis they have on under them. I shake my head. After last night, I am not sure I ever could again. "Why not? Don't you want to swim?"

I want to trust this guy with the feelings fresh from the dream, but I do not really know him. I try to turn my fear into a joke. "Nope. I had a dream once." Last night. "Where I was killed just for wearing a swimsuit." I laugh.

His gaze snaps to me. He doesn't say anything at first. He lifts his hand and taps twice on my back, right where it meets my neck with just one finger. "I doubt it was because you were wearing a swimsuit, but it explains what took you so long."

Not sure what he meant about the last part because I am starting to freak out about him knowing where my birthmark is. Before I could say anything, I remember the dream. Maybe Anna had been correct. They very well may be memories, not merely dreams. I think I would rather they be dreams. But then again, this sexy beast is now standing in front of me.

He just smiles at me. We meet up with the others, well, not the beta couple. They were walking behind us hand in hand. They never left my side. I took the bag I had carried from the car and set it on the ground. I took out the towel I had brought and laid it on the ground while the others were talking about the water.

Hunter sat down next to me in the sand. I guess he wasn't swimming either. Considering he was wearing his leather chaps, he wasn't dressed for it.

"So, where did you grow up this time?" Hunter asks, I'm guessing to break the ice and give us something to talk about.

I look over my shoulder to see that the betas have sat down on a towel just like us, but they are both on alert. They are close but far enough away that we could talk freely.

I turn back to Hunter. "A smaller area in Missouri."

He nods. "You are Rose and Robert's granddaughter. That means your dad is Robbie. You were right under my nose all this time."

Of course he would know my dad. My father grew up at the Farm. "Yes. My dad met my mother, Carol, who lived in Missouri, in an even smaller town than I grew up in, but they decided to settle down in Cape when they got pregnant with me."

He nods again and then starts to pepper me with questions. I even get a few in of my own. We sit there talking the entire time our friends are in the water. Just getting to know one another. He says that we have been together in other lifetimes, and according to my dreams, I believe him.

There is just something about sitting there talking with him that is getting to me. I have never had such an instant connection with anyone like this. I make friends easily, but this is even different from that. Deeper.

The guys didn't stay in the water long. They rejoin us on the beach. We eat the lunch we had brought. It is just simple: sandwiches and water bottles. Even sandwiches and water are better when he is on the beach with me.

After we eat, we pack everything back up. We're all going to a museum. Then, heading back to the Farm. As we get back to the cars, Hunter looks up at me. "Want to ride?" he asks as he indicates the bike.

I start to say yes, want to say yes, but don't know if I should. I look at Anna, and she was already nodding. I looked at the betas. They are there to protect me anyway. Emily just shrugs and looks at Jameson. "Stay between the cars," Jameson tells Hunter.

Hunter nods, then hands me his helmet. I put it on, then climb on the bike behind him. At first, I put a bit of distance between us, but he wasn't having any of that. He grabs hold of both of my knees and drags me across the seat. I am now pressed tight against his back, my thighs hugging his hips. I could feel my nipples harden and pebble against his back.

The feel of my hardened nipples against the leather jacket is enough to make me want more, for the first time in my life. I am an eighteen-year-old virgin. That is one of the things I can say I am proud of. Even with the peer pressure I got throughout high school, I stood my ground.

The reason, however, is that not once have I been turned on enough to take things further than a simple kiss. Don't get me wrong, I can and have been attracted to features, but never enough. I was starting to think there was something wrong with that part of my body. Being on this bike, with my body wrapped so tightly around this man, I know I had been incorrect, or rather, it had been with the wrong person.

Hunter reaches back once more, taking my hands. He kisses each one, which set the butterflies loose in my stomach, then placed them both on his rock-hard stomach. How did one get abs that hard? I could feel the ridges of his muscles right through his t-shirt.

He hesitates for a moment, then starts the bike. Oh, the rumble! He pulls out behind Emily, following closely. "Are you right back there?" he asks, but I don't answer. I don't think I am able to. I feel him laugh, then he makes his way back to the ferry.

The ferry ride back is even better the second time. I have never been so comfortable with someone before. I like just talking to him. The things he says, the silliest things really, would make me laugh. There is something about him. So, when he asks if I want to go out just the two of us, I automatically say yes. I wasn't asking anyone for permission this time.

The museum was fun. Heck, the entire day has been fun. I really needed a little fun. Ever since my birthday, there has been nothing but duty. I end up riding back to the Farm on the back of Hunter's bike.

Once we are out of the city, Hunter drops one hand down to rest on top of mine and just leaves it there. I don't move. I like the attention, probably more than I should.

By the time we get back to the Farm, it takes me a moment for my legs to stop vibrating. Hunter just laughs at me. It isn't like he was making fun of me. But I guess my facial expressions are humorous. "You will get used to it," he tells me. Would I be on his bike enough to get used to it?

When I am able to walk, I start toward the house. "I need to go see my grandmother," I tell him. He comes with me. When I get to the hall, I turn to go to the conference room.

Hunter stops with a look of confusion on his face. "Rose's office is this way," he tells me, pointing to the other hall. I shake my head. "Not anymore, or not right now anyway. She has set up in the conference room."

I lead the way.

"I wonder why she did that," he muses aloud. "She has always had her office in the other hall. The conference room was only used for privacy."

I nod but don't say anything. I reached up to hit the button on the intercom. Almost instantly, I hear a "Yes, you can come in," my grandmother says to the little box on the wall. I open the door and walk in. While we were gone, the room had changed. The long table that was the only thing in the room before has been turned around to make room for a whole living room suite on the other side.

There is a couch and a love seat as well as a desk. My grandmother is currently sitting at the desk. I make my way over to the couch. Sitting down, I look to my Granny. "That was just what the doctor ordered."

She laughs at me. "I see you are home and brought a friend," she looks up at Hunter. "Thank you for coming. I know you had other plans, and we appreciate you making the time for us. Please have a seat," she motions to the chair in front of her desk.

Hunter does what she says, but looks right at me when he speaks. "It was definitely my pleasure," he smiles, then turns his attention back to my grandmother.

She looks between us. "What did I miss?" she asks. I shrug. I don't know what is happening between Hunter and me, but there is something. It is something big.

She shakes her head and picks up a piece of paper from beside her. "Do you know what a non-disclosure agreement is, Mr. Riggs?" she asks him as she hands a piece of paper across the desk. There is already a pen sitting there.

He picks up the paper, skims over it, then sets it back down. "What is this about? Why would I need a nondisclosure? I thought you needed help with a new shifter. Why would I need discretion?" he looks down at the paper, then raises his eyes to me.

Granny claps her hands in front of her, smiling up at Hunter. "I know this is unusual. This is just not how things are done, but there are some things that we will need to speak about that I don't want outside of this room."

Hunter says nothing for a moment. I can see the confusion written all over his face. "Does this have anything to do with the beta couple following us around today?"

Granny nods. "Yes, but that is all I can say for now." She looks back at me, then back at him. Hunter follows her line of sight and just looks at me for a moment. He turns back to the paper in front of him. Picking up the pen, he scribbles on the paper, then sets the pen back down.

Granny picks up the paper and stores it in her desk. "Thank you, Mr. Riggs," she says at the same time that he asks, "Is this because she is your granddaughter?"

She chuckles. "That is one reason. When would you like to start?" she asks, changing the subject.

"We can start now. By the way, I should say I plan to date your granddaughter. Just to keep things transparent," he stands and holds his hand out to me. I smile and take his hand. We walk out together.

Once we were out in the hall, with the conference room door closed behind us, Hunter turns to me. "We will grab something to eat on the way to the training grounds. There shouldn't be too many people there," he says, and starts walking again.

CHAPTER SIXTEEN

Hunter

"U m... about that." She hesitates. "We cannot use the training grounds."

Now it is my turn to hesitate. I open my mouth to ask... something... I am not even sure what at this point. I have so many questions and nowhere near enough answers. The math is simply not adding up.

I do not know what is going on with the love of my life, but something is definitely going on. "We need a bit more privacy." She adds. That only adds to my ever-growing list of questions.

When we finish up our initial training session, I will be looking into what's going on around here. I can't help but feel as if I am being lied to. And coming from the raven-haired beauty in front of me, it hurts that much more.

Then she goes and throws me off once again by raising her eyebrows suggestively at me. I give her a small smile. I know deep down, though, I will not allow myself to touch my fated mate like that until she knows without a doubt who we are to each other. Doing so before then would feel too much like taking advantage of her.

After grabbing some food from the serving hall, we make our way to the ATV hut. Handing her my own plate to hold while I drive, I take us deep into the property. All the way to the rear to make sure that we are far enough away from anyone, and that will give her the privacy that she wants.

"What happened with the other trainer?" I ask her as we park the ATV. "Rose did say another was here, didn't she?"

She swallows her food, and I cannot help but watch as her elegant throat works, but then she gets an irritated look on her face that completely ruins the visual. "Yes. Nathan was here. Ugh, I can't stand him."

"What happened?" I repeat, because if that little fuck did anything to hurt my mate, I would tear his throat out.

"First, I absolutely did not like his attitude. He snapped his fingers in my face like I was a fucking dog. That was the very first time I met him." She pauses to take a drink from the water bottle in her hand. "Then we come out here, and he still has the attitude, but he did show me how to shift. Once I do, he splits, taking the ATV with him and leaving me out here in my animal form. I had absolutely no idea how to change back. I was stuck."

"What the hell?" I knew that Nathan was a prick. That is the reason I am always so busy; no one wants to work with him at all. That could explain why Rose was so desperate, but it makes me want to hunt him down and end him just for upsetting my mate. He'd better be glad he didn't physically hurt her, or I would.

She nods and takes another bite of her sandwich, but she is still fuming.

Her anger is still palpable, and I cannot handle it any longer. "What do you shift into this time?" I ask, changing the subject off the dickhead. I did not even realize that I had mixed the past with the present once again until she raises her brow at the way it was worded.

She giggles. Oh, how I love that sound. "What would you like me to change into this time?"

"Wait... what do you mean?" There was no way she could choose. You get one animal. Whatever the animal is that you shift into at your moonlight ceremony is the animal you are stuck with... no matter what. It is normally a good match for the human, but there is still only one.

I shake my head. There is no way. "Can you really pick?" The way she nods enthusiastically, she really does believe that she can pick. Didn't her grandparents explain these things to her? "Tiger," I say simply. I am hoping that is what she is again. "That is what you were when we were together last." I miss that lifetime; even though we died young, we died together.

With a bright smile, she sets down her plate and jumps off the ATV. She turns around to face away from me to start undressing. However, the look she shoots over her shoulder at me makes the blood rush, and the crotch of my pants is suddenly a lot tighter.

When she turns back around, I readjust myself. When she is completely naked and her cute, tight little ass is on display just for me, she starts to shift.

I watch as little orange and black hairs start to appear on her bare skin. The shape of her body soon follows. She drops to the ground as a beautiful tigress and turns back to face me.

As her gaze lands on the front of my pants, something happens. The orange stripes start to spasm, switching back and forth between orange and black, then from stripes to whirls, before disappearing into a different cat completely. My jaw drops, and I can only stare.

She still has the head of a cat; however, it is now broader with a sleek, muscular body that is covered in short, slick, black fur, and I can faintly see charcoal gray rosettes. They are so faint that if I weren't looking for them, they would almost disappear.

The magnificent beast's eyes shimmer with red and yellow, reminding me of flames. That couldn't be right. She couldn't have flames in her eyes—eyes that happened to be looking at me with a razor-sharp focus that lifted the hairs on the back of my nape.

"*Oh shit.*" I hear Cadence's voice even though that is an impossibility.

I stand there and just stare for so long. This explains...everything. It changes everything.

I take a few cautious steps toward her. "Oh baby. I am so happy for you," I whisper. "I am honored to stand at your side."

I stand again and reach behind me, grabbing the collar of my shirt. I pull it off and then turn my back before dropping my pants. I shift into the only animal I have. A tiger. One so dark that it will blend into the very darkness itself when needed. I turned to face my love with my blue eyes, looking straight into her flame-colored ones.

I step back up to her just as she changes back into the tiger I had seen before. I then set off at a pace that we can still enjoy while playing. This is the first time in over twenty-five years we have been able to run together. I am going to make sure she enjoys every second.

CHAPTER SEVENTEEN

Cadence

W E RUN TOGETHER SIDE by side for a long time. Our tigers play together like they have always been together. When we make our way back, hours later, to the ATV, it is completely dark outside. I shift back with almost no effort.

The events of the day, combined with hours of play as a tiger, left me completely exhausted. I lay right there on the ground, not caring that I am naked with a stranger. A stranger I happened to have a complicated past with.

Hunter is doing the same right beside me. I look over to find him watching me once again. We just lay there in silence, staring into one another's eyes. Eventually, slowly, giving me plenty of time to pull away if I want to, he pulls me to him and places his lips against mine. Sweetly. Softly.

At first, it is just that, a soft, sweet peck. Soon, the kiss becomes harder and more intense. I gasp at the sensations surging through my body. He takes advantage, and his tongue plunges into my mouth to tangle with my own.

I lean into him, wrapping my arms around his neck. As the length of my body comes to rest against his, I can feel the entire length of his erection pressing against my own flesh.

That's when Hunter, all too soon, pulls back. "We'd better get dressed," his voice is almost a whisper. "If we don't, things will happen that you are not ready for yet." He leans in once again and takes possession of my mouth, only to pull away once more. This time, he rolls onto his back and covers his face with his hands. He screams, but it is muffled due to his hands.

I tell myself not to look, but I can't stop myself from dragging my gaze down his body. From his gorgeous face to the well-defined muscles, to the impressive erection that stands tall and proud. His arousal for me is on clear display. There is no hiding it. Movement from Hunter causes my gaze to move back to his face.

I look away. I am completely embarrassed to be caught looking at him. I jump up, going straight for my clothes. I keep my back turned away from him, even though all his nakedness was just pressed against my own nakedness. The fact that I was caught looking at him just set us back another step.

My embarrassment alone kept me turned away from him long after I had pulled my clothes back on. What is happening? I have never acted like this. The only thing I could guess is that it had to do with the person I am with. The combination of the here and now added fuel to the fire of the dream me. If that wasn't it, I am going completely insane. Weird.

Divine happiness runs through me in an instant, as Hunter walks up behind me and wraps his now fully clothed arms around me. He rests his head on my shoulder just like he did in the dream. "I'm sorry, love. I didn't mean for that to happen yet," he kisss my cheek, then he steps away.

I feel cold and lacking without his touch, despite the heat, but I will never show it. Pulling my big girl panties up, I turn around and face him with my chin held high. "Oh my God. There is nothing to apologize for," I tell him. I make my way to the ATV and climb into the driver's seat. "It's my turn to drive this bad boy," since the other is off limits.

He just smiles and climbs in. I drive all the way around the compound just wanting to be with him a little longer. I then make my way back to the garage. It is surprisingly quiet the entire way back. Neither of us say anything. When I park, I turn to face him. "When do you need me again?"

He whispers something I almost didn't catch. As it was, I pretended I didn't hear the whispered "always." "Right after breakfast will be fine."

He leans in slowly, once again kissing me on the cheek before climbing out of the ATV. "Good night, Cadence," he says as he walks out of the little building's side door.

I didn't sit there long. I gave him just enough time to get to his room. I'm not sure exactly what is going on between us, but things are moving awfully fast in some ways, and not enough in others. Sighing, I make my way to my room. It takes me a while to fall asleep, but when I do, another dream is waiting for me.

This time, I am a bit older than I am presently, closer to Hunter's age. I am standing in what appears to be a church. There are white flowers everywhere. I am standing next to an unknown man who looks a little like my father.

I am wearing a beautiful wedding dress. The dress is stunning. Strapless, sweetheart neckline, that is made of silky material that goes all the way to the floor with a beaded bottom creating beautiful flowers. The delicate flowers started at my knees and ran the entire length of the train that was spread out behind me. I could not see the shoes even though I could feel myself wearing some extremely high heels. The straps crossed across my feet and slightly higher up my ankle.

The music starts from the other room, it is the wedding march. Signaling that it is time to move. The man standing next to me offers me his arm. "Are you ready, sweetheart?" I don't answer him but take his arm without hesitation.

The doors we were facing opened before us, giving us a view of the church. The pews on both sides were full of people. They were turned in their seats to watch the bride walk down the aisle. On each pew, set a beautiful bouquet of the same white flowers that I was holding in my hand. There were three women standing on the left side of the preacher and four men standing on the right. The preacher was smiling at me, but I only had eyes for the groom.

Hunter stood there tall and proud. He was utterly happy to be standing there waiting for his bride. Love was shining through his every pore. As I reached the front of the church, he took my hand. I handed the flowers off to the maid of honor, who looked exactly like Anna. The dream me doesn't hesitate, though.

I turned back to Hunter as the preacher started. "We are gathered here today to join these two shifters into a holy union that only our kind can become." He looks around the church. "Is there anyone here today who is opposed to this union? Please speak now or forever hold your peace."

Just then, the doors at the back of the church burst open. A woman with long, natural orange-red curly hair steps into the church. She is followed by three men. "I object!" she screams.

Felicia, the evil witch, was here to stop her wedding. Three others stepped into the room behind them. The potions are ready. That was seven altogether. At once, they all threw potions in every direction. Explosions went off where the potions dropped, stunning everyone and causing chaos.

I shifted right there, tearing through my beautiful wedding gown. Seconds later, in the place of the bride stood a lioness with her groom lion by her side. Together, they rushed forward to charge into action. However, before the lions could reach their targets, I was jolted awake.

It took me a moment to pull myself from the dream world. I am lying in my bed, at the Farm, in complete lioness form. I look up to find Hunter standing over me. He is holding a single red rose. *"What are you doing here?"* I ask, as he shouldn't be in my room. I try not to be snarky, but after yet another dream with him front and center, I am a little off.

Shock appears on his face, but it is gone in a second. "You can speak in animal form?" He pauses. "...of course you can," he laughs, rubbing both hands across his face. "When you didn't show up to breakfast, I got worried," he answers my question from before.

He looks over my lioness form, which I didn't even know I had. "What was it this time?" he asks, but I don't tell him everything.

"Felicia and her minions." Choosing just to tell him what caused the shift, not the memory before.

He knows that it's always Felicia. "Can you change back?" he asks after everything that had happened the day before and the dream I just woke from. I am not sure I want him to see me naked so soon. My adrenaline is still extremely high. *"I will wait a few more minutes. Can I meet you in the courtyard?"*

Disappointment flashes across his face, but it is only a flash. He nods and walks out of my room after placing the rose on the stand next to my bed. As soon as he is gone, I shift back and dress as fast as I can. I believe it is time to talk to the one person who might know what is going on. My grandmother: I pick up the rose and carry it with me.

I make my way to the conference room, thinking about what I am going to say. I bring the rose to my nose to inhale its heavenly aroma. Roses are my favorite.

I need help, but I am not sure how to ask. I know what I am feeling, in addition to all the dreams that are really memories of past lives.

When I reach my grandmother's new office, the door is standing open. Emily is sitting on a low seat with my granny at her desk. I come in and flop down on the couch. I know I was already late, but that doesn't matter, though. This is important.

"Good afternoon, Cadence." The beta female greets me. "Pretty flower." She is once again wearing the black-on-black uniform. I look down at my own clothing and notice that we match. Since black is my favorite color, I normally wore the same colors.

I echo her greetings, then turn to face my granny. "I need help," I state, still not knowing what to say. I just stick with the truth. I would deal with the embarrassment later. I started by filling them in on all the dreams. "According to Anna, I am starting to get my memories by way of dreams."

My grandmother sets down whatever she was working on and joins me on the couch. "That is normally how it happens," she smiles sympathetically. "What is the problem?" I look down at my hands. "Well, every single night since my first shift, I have been having dreams. While these dreams are always in a different setting, even a different time. Every single one of them, except one, has been just one thing every dream has in common."

She just waits but has a knowing smile on her face. I look over to Emily, and she has the exact same look on her face. "Hunter," I state. "It's not that he is just there; it's the feeling I have for him in the dreams that is affecting the here and now. I know that I have just met him in this lifetime, but the feelings I have had in the past are invading my head and heart today."

Granny nods. "Well, there is a story. I won't use the word legend; I know you don't like that term." She smiles again. "Have you ever heard of a fated mate?"

I shake my head, so she goes on. "A fated mate is a single person who is meant for a shifter. This person is said to be almost half of the shift or soul. No matter what life brings, a shifter, this one person is always there, with or without memories."

I think about that. The thought of Hunter being my fated mate settled nicely in my heart. It feels like it belongs there. It also confuses me more. "So, you're saying that, because of this bond, as being fated mates, that I couldn't fight these feelings I am having for a virtual stranger?"

"That's correct. If Hunter is truly your fated mate, and that's what it sounds like to me, then every single life cycle, you two would have met and will always fall in love. The goddess has a funny way of showing her power sometimes."

"Jameson and I..." Emily starts. "Were only preteens when we met in this life cycle. Within a week, even without our memories, we were madly in love with each other. We knew we would spend the rest of our lives together. Turns out lifetimes." She smiles fondly at her memories.

I nod to them both. They have given me a lot to think about. I sit there in silence doing just that for a while. I don't really know what I want to do about this gift the Goddess has given me yet. I would be a little crazier than I thought if I gave it up. If that was even possible. The thought of never seeing Hunter again hurt me in a place so deep that I never even knew existed.

"Oh... I should also mention that Anna knows about me. She heard me screaming one night. When I was dying in a dream. She rushed in and found me in my panther form. She was brave enough to even wake me up." Strangely, this knowledge didn't seem to surprise her.

I wonder if Anna has already said something. After all, my grandmother is her employer. "I guess if she hasn't said anything yet, she isn't going to," she laughs. "You still need to be careful at least until your memories finish coming in."

I glance up at the clock on the wall. I suppose I should get going soon. I am already going to be eating lunch instead of breakfast. I stand up. "I'd better get going," even though I wasn't sure I really wanted to. "I am already a little bit late. Only by about 3 hours." I walk through the doors and turn back once more. "Love you, see you later."

I am on my way to burn up some pent-up energy. Hopefully, my memories will come soon and answer some of these burning questions I have. Until then, it is time to go meet my fate.

CHAPTER EIGHTEEN

Hunter

"ALRIGHT, CADENCE," I SAY to get her attention. This is our first official training session. "I like to start off slower on the first day of training. So don't think that this is what we will do every day."

We are currently in the training area, which is located right behind the house. Since we will not be shifting until after lunch, we can start over here. This also gives the others a chance to see part of her training. If they don't see any training whatsoever, then people will start asking questions that we are not ready for.

"All right, let's do this," she says, starting to bounce on her toes. She is excited now, but probably won't be after hours of running.

"One of the most important aspects of training or even battle is stamina. A good way to build stamina is to run." I smile at her groan. "It's important to know when to fight and when to run, but it's even more important to be able to run if needed. So, let's get started."

The first two laps around the training area were at a slow jog. On the third lap, we pick up speed. Every few laps after that, we would speed up again.

We only run about twenty laps before I start to slow us back down again. Cadence collapses on the ground. We are finally finished. I laugh and sit next to her. "It's not fun, is it?" I laugh again. "Tomorrow will be worse."

She pouts at me and shakes her head. She is still trying to catch her breath, and it's the cutest thing ever. I love this woman so much. Always have and always will. The goddess made sure of that.

After so many lifetimes, or even just one, I cannot help but love her. Maybe just maybe, with her being the Black Dawn, we can finally defeat the evil Felicia and get our happily ever after. After all this time, we are due. You would think, anyway.

I let Lizzie... I mean, Cadence—I have to stop using her old name—rest for twenty minutes, then take her through a few self-defense moves. I make sure she has every move mastered before moving on to the next.

When it was time for lunch, I let her go to her room to shower, and I did the same. I instructed her to wear her robe this time so she would be able to shift. I can already tell that it is going to be torture. Until her memories come in, I get to watch my love get undressed many times and not be able to touch her.

Yes, for shape-shifters, nudity is common, and it is considered rude to get aroused or even to really look at another naked shifter like that. However, it is completely different when it comes to one's fated mate.

The day I stop getting hot and bothered by the sight of her is the day you end this life cycle and let me try again.

Once we are back in the same place as the day before, we get out of the ATV and stand facing each other.

"All right, I have only seen you shift from human to animal once, but that one time was sloppy." She starts to open her mouth, but I cut her off. "I understand you are a new baby, and that is to be expected."

"The fact is, with your position, you need to always be ready. Now you may hate me a little when we are done here..."

"I could never hate you," she cuts in.

I give her a small smile because I know she is going to be exhausted by the time we are finished here today. Too many shifts can turn anyone's mood sour. "I want you to pick an animal in your large arsenal, not the panther, and shift to that."

From the little I saw yesterday, I feel as if she is having trouble concentrating on the final moments of her shift and reverting to her natural form. If she was a normal shifter, this wouldn't be a problem.

She nods and removes her robe. Seeing her standing there completely naked, and not being able to touch her, is killing me. All I want to do is wrap her in my arms and sink myself deep. I just want to go home.

Cadence shifts into the tiger but once again loses focus and goes back to the panther. She has no issues changing animals once she is in panther form but cannot skip the baseline animal altogether.

"Back to human, my love." Once she is fully human once again, I give her a moment before telling her to do it again. After the third time, I stop her.

"Is it just the tiger?" I ask. "Have you tried a different one?"

She pants on the grass in front of me. I sit down beside her and pull her into my lap. She starts to protest, but I don't allow that. I don't care that she is naked and covered in grass and dirt.

"I don't know what I'm doing wrong," she tells me.

I rub my hand down her hair, clearing the clumps of dirt from her midnight strands. "Why don't we try a different tactic? Try changing into the panther from the start."

"Are we not trying to keep that from happening?" she asks.

"Have you even tried to do just the panther?" I counter.

She thinks about this for a second, then shakes her head. "I am not sure how many more shifts I have in me, but I will try."

She moves off my lap but does not stand. She is already getting tired. She has the cutest look of determination in her jade green eyes. When she shifts this time, she does exactly as I expected. She shifts straight into the panther. No hesitation. "Good girl," I tell her right before she passes out.

It takes her a good ten minutes to automatically shift back to human. I slip her robe back on and pick her up. I place a small kiss on the top of her head, then take her to her room. I dig into my pocket, and place the small black velvet-clad box on her nightstand. I leave her to rest once I have her tucked into her bed. One day soon, I will be able to lie right there beside her and watch over her. That day is not today, though, so I quietly step away from the bed.

CHAPTER NINETEEN

Cadence

I WAKE THE NEXT morning to find a small black box in the same spot that Hunter had placed the rose yesterday. I open the box to find the most beautiful necklace I have ever seen. It is silver and moonstone. The moonstone is wrapped in silver wire with tiny leaves that look as if they were hand-carved a very long time ago.

I pull the necklace from the velvet and hold it up to the light. Somehow this necklace feels familiar to me. Like it belongs to me, or did at one time. I want nothing more than to put it on right this instant, but I know I will be shifting and that would not be smart. Against my better judgement, I place it back into the box. I hide the box in my closet then start getting myself ready for another long day of training.

For the next week, it was the same thing. I would wake early to find some small gift waiting for me. I know they are all from Hunter. There has been anything from roses to the jewelry to some of my favorite snacks. Every single time, I get a deep sense of belonging, of being loved, of just being thought about on a daily basis.

Every little touch magnified that feeling tenfold. The littlest things would set off the butterflies in my chest. They are no longer just in my belly. So spending so much time training with him was heaven and hell at the same time.

He works my body so hard that I am completely exhausted by the end of the day. There is almost no time for anything else. The time together did, however, let us get to know each other. In this lifetime. The little things that make up a person's whole. I could see how I kept falling in love with this man because just a week after he has arrived, I am smitten. Well on my way to being head over heels for him.

Each evening, we would spend time without friends before returning to our own rooms for sleep. Every night, I would dream. Another memory and another life cycle. Each one was full of danger, blood, and death. That and Hunter were the only common trends.

I went to bed one night, and for the first time in a while, I did not dream. Not at all. I woke the next morning knowing exactly what and who I am.

Waking with so much information flowing through my head is a bizarre sensation. I lay there for a long time, not even moving, just going through all the memories. All the life cycles I have lived. All the knowledge I have learned over the years.

When I went to bed last night, I still had more questions than answers. Now, I have most of those answers. And even answers to questions I didn't even know to ask. I knew now not to question the legend or even my relationship with Hunter.

Glancing at the clock on my bedside table, it informs me it is just after five o'clock in the morning. It is still early even for shifter standards. Most of the shifters don't start to get up until six, except a select few, Hunter being one.

As I lay there, going through all the lifecycles I have lived, I decide to surprise him. I know that he has held out from really touching me. Held out on being with me. All because I did not have my memories yet. Now I know without a doubt that Hunter is mine. I won't let that stop us anymore.

I jump out of bed, not even bothering to dress. There is no need. I slip into my robe, which is now mostly used to shift, and I tie the sash as I slip out of my bedroom door. I tiptoe down the quiet halls. I am trying my best not to wake anyone else.

When I get to Hunter's room, I don't bother to knock. I want my early morning visit to be a surprise. Announcing my presence would ruin that. As I close the door behind me, I notice that the room is empty. I do hear the shower running in the next room, though. Perfect.

I do not hesitate. I make my way across the room. When I get to the door that I know will lead to the bathroom, since this room is an exact copy of my own, I enter the bathroom quietly. The door is already ajar, letting steam out into the bedroom, so it doesn't make a sound. As I enter, I freeze.

I search the small room for my mate. His bathroom is a mirror of mine, just like his bedroom. Hunter's back is to me, and his head is under the spray of water. That is probably why he doesn't notice me yet.

Between the steam filling the room and the heavenly scent of my mate mixed with the smell of his shampoo, I am lost for a moment. I watch as the suds and soapy water are rinsed from his hair, leaving a trail right down his back and over the curve of his backside.

I pull the sash of my robe, dropping the entire thing right there where I stand, still in the doorway of the room. I step forward while he is still distracted with the simple act. I slip in behind him, right as he starts to step back out of the spray of water, bringing his back right against the front of my body. I slip my hands around his waist, running them up the smooth, wet, slick hardness that is his body. No clothes separate us this time. I lean in to place a light kiss on his spine, letting the water flow over my own head, as I run my hands from his waist up to his pecs.

Hunter lets out a sigh of contentment. He knows what my being here in the shower with him means. He leans back a little, relaxing into me. He lets me run my hands over his slick body without saying a word. No words are said because, in this moment, no words are needed.

Testing my limits, I let my hands slide lower, slowly over each one of the ridges that make up his washboard abs, right over his happy trail, down to the erection that I know will be there. I find him eager for my touch, just as eager as I am to touch him.

I fist his hardness, right at the very end of him, letting my hand slowly lower all the way to the base. When my fist meets flesh, I let it glide right back to the tip, before starting again.

Hunter only allows me to do this a few times before he is growling. He gently removes my hand before he turns in my arms to face me. Framing my face, he leans into me. There is no other for this man, no matter the lifetime. There is so much love shining in his eyes, and it is all for me. I only see it for a fraction of a second before his mouth is covering my own.

The water pours over our heads as his lips hit mine, but that doesn't stop us. He devours my lips. Stepping into me, he presses me back with his own body, until my back is pressed up against the cool tiles of the shower wall.

As my back hits the wall, we both gasp at the same time, opening to the exploration of tongues. When neither of us can breathe any longer without coming up for air, Hunter leans back a fraction. "Hello, love."

With a smile, he lowers his head again, this time not going straight to my lips; he softly kisses the corner of my mouth, then my cheek, making a trail of kisses from my mouth to my neck. I tilt my head over and back to give him more access. He doesn't stay there long, making his way down to my breast, which he grabs onto, squeezing gently. He pinches my nipples only to kiss each one to remove the sting.

He makes his way back up the same trail that he took before. Taking my mouth in yet another searing, heated kiss. I wrap my arms around his neck, pulling him even closer.

He runs his hands down my back until he grabs hold of a cheek of my ass in each hand. He lifts me in the air, shoving my back into the wall of the shower. He never breaks the kiss.

I wrap my legs around his waist. As I do, I can feel the head of his cock resting right at the edge of my opening. Without hesitation, I press my hips down a little harder onto him, making him slip inside of me. We both groan.

Even though this body is a virgin, that doesn't mean that my mind is. I know exactly what I want, and I know how to get it. With the water and my tight virgin opening, I must wiggle a little to get his large cock to slip further inside of me. Hunter lets me go at my own pace. He never breaks the passionate kiss.

When my downward motion meets hesitation, I stop. I know this will hurt; it won't last long, but it will hurt. I raise my body back up off him a couple of times, just a little, to get more of my own personal brand of lube to help coat the path. The water around us doesn't help in situations like this; it only makes it harder.

Rising one last time, I thrust my body downwards at the same time as Hunter thrusts up, breaking through the innocence of this body. I gasp as the sensation hits. Neither of us is moving until I am ready once again. Taking my time, I let my body adjust to the invasion of something so big being inside of me.

As I slowly start to move again, Hunter must decide that he has given me long enough because he starts to thrust up into me harder. My moan is swallowed up by his mouth that is still on my own. In this position, he is hitting the secret spot that hides deep inside of me, making me come hard and fast.

Not letting up, Hunter pushes me through the orgasm and the aftershocks that come with it, bringing me right back up again. As I come for the second time in such a short span, Hunter finally allows himself to follow. I can feel the hot jets of his seed as it is pumped right into my body.

We stand there, still locked in each other's arms, just catching our breaths. As my heart rate comes back to normal, Hunter moves backwards, pulling me with him, bringing us both back under the surprisingly still hot water.

Once we are clean and dried off, thanks to his attentive care, we lie down together in his bed. It had been years since we had been able to lie together and snuggle, lifetimes really, so that's what we did, with little kisses here and touches there.

After an hour or so, I pull back slightly and ask, "Do we need to continue training?"

He just smiles at me. "I have some training for you to do." He pulls me on top of him as he pulls my face down to his, kissing me deeply. He reaches his hand between our bodies and positions himself at my entrance.

As I slide down on him once again, I let out a moan that is mixed with a sigh. I will never get enough of this, no matter how many lifetimes we spend together. My mate means everything to me.

I thrust myself down on him, seating myself completely. It has only been an hour or so, but my body already needs time to relax around him. Rotating my hips in a circle, once my body's own lubricant starts to work again. I lift my hips up off him just to bring them back down at the same time as he thrusts up into me, hitting the most delicious spot.

I lean back slightly, breaking the kiss just to get a deeper angle. As he makes his way down my body, he is leaving little kisses in his wake. Each one in his hands, he takes the right nipple into his mouth, suckling. I rise, and he chases my body with his mouth. The leverage I need sends me spiraling into another life-altering orgasm.

I rock my body slowly, working through the aftershocks. He releases my nipples, but he keeps thrusting into me until the last of my aftershocks dissipate. He flips us over, somehow never making our bodies lose contact.

He works me slowly first, then harder with each thrust, bringing yet another orgasm to the surface. This time we explode together. We collapse on the bed side by side. We do not even move for the longest time. We both need to just lie here and try not to die.

Hunter places a slight kiss on my lips before pulling me in close. We lay there in each other's arms, and it was not long before we were both fast asleep.

CHAPTER TWENTY

Cadence

WHO KNOWS HOW MUCH later, we are woken by a knock on the door. Neither of us have moved much at all. We have only adjusted our positions to curl into each other, not bothering with the blankets. We are content to use each other's body heat.

"Hey, Hunter..." I hear the beta's voice at the same time the doorknob rattles. Not even allowing Hunter to answer, he opens the door and steps in. At least the hall behind him is empty. "Robert sent me... Oh shit!" He stops in his tracks.

I look around the room with new eyes. The bed that had been neatly made a few hours ago is now rumpled under our naked bodies.

Hunter and I face each other, our lower halves pressed together, legs tangled. Thankfully, with the way we are positioned, the beta could see very little, just a hint of a breast.

The room itself was almost untouched, except the air smells of sweat and sex. Neither of us could deny what had happened here, even if we wanted to. I knew, for a fact, that neither of us would ever do such a thing to our fated mates.

It took only seconds for Jameson to figure out what was going on. I think I catch a smirk on his face as he turns his back, but I can't be sure. "I guess I know what held you up," he chuckles to himself. "I'll let him know you'll be a few minutes." He leaves, pulling the door closed behind him. I could still hear his laughter as he made his way down the hall.

Hunter sighs. "I guess we'd better get up," he states, but does not move. Instead, he pulls me closer and places soft lips on mine. It does not take much to coax him into deepening the kiss.

All too soon, he pulls back. "Later, love..." He kisses the tip of my nose before rising from the bed. "I promise," he assures me, heading to the closet. A few minutes later, he emerges fully dressed, carrying a stack of clothes, which he set on the edge of the bed.

"Fine," I grumble, but get up. Hunter sits to pull on his boots while I pick up the pile of clothes.

In the stack is a pair of sweats and a T-shirt. I slip them on without underwear; I will need to go back to my room to at least get a bra. I could not go without that.

When the bedroom door closes behind us, Hunter leans down to kiss me sweetly before we part ways. He is going to see my grandfather, and I am headed to my room. I do not want to be in that room for that conversation; I would wait until the anger cooled.

I decide to take a quick shower to wash away the evidence of our lovemaking. In a house full of shifters, cleaning up a little is necessary.

By the time I finish, Hunter has finished with Grandpa. He does not comment on anything that was said. He comes into my room as I step out of the bathroom with a towel wrapped around me, smiling as he watches.

Instead of disappearing into the closet like him, I pick out my clothes and return to the bedroom naked. I dress slowly, knowing he is watching.

"What are we doing today?" I ask as I slide my panties over my hips.

His gaze never leaves me, but he answers. I smirk, but he doesn't notice. "We are leaving."

I pause fastening my bra to stare at him. I do not want to leave the Farm for good, now that my memories are back. I know I am needed here more than ever. Still, I will follow my fated mate anywhere. "What?" I squeak.

His gaze snaps to mine. "Not forever," he chuckles. "We're going for a lunch date." His smile, reserved just for me, made me want to remove the clothing I had just put on, and he knows it.

"Alone?" I ask. He nods, his eyes falling once again to my breasts as I hook the bra clips. The idea of getting away from the Farm with Hunter alone thrills me.

So much so that the sexy tease is forgotten. I throw on the clothes as fast as I can. The sooner I am ready, the sooner we could leave. We were alone now, but it is different when the house and property are always full of people who could hear and smell better than most.

We make our way to his bike. He must have found or bought another helmet because he hands me one that is black with a little glitter. I slip it on and fasten the strap. Once he is on the bike, I climb behind him.

This time, I don't hesitate to pull as close as possible, wrapping my arms around his waist. He rumbles, and I hum in response. He chuckles at my reaction.

We leave the Farm property and head first to a town we had passed before but never visited. Texas City, Texas, is bigger than I expected. Hunter steers us to a place called Momma's.

Momma's is a small diner right at the edge of town. If you didn't know it was there, you'd probably miss it completely. Inside, it has a quaint, old-school charm. Memorabilia lines the walls, capturing attention in every corner. If not for holding Hunter's hand, I might have still been standing at the door.

Once seated, Hunter hands me a menu but does not take one himself.

"What's good here? Looks like you've been here before."

He smiles. "About three years ago, I stumbled upon this place while training a lion shifter."

I hand him back the menu. "Order for me then," I tell him as the server approaches. She has short, spiky brown hair and several facial piercings. If her hair was darker, I might have called her emo.

"Welcome to Momma's!" she greets, her chipper voice mismatched with the exterior. "What can I get you started with?"

Hunter orders two signature burgers, sweet potato fries, and two half-cut sweet teas. Once she leaves, he turns his attention back to me. "You told me that first day that you died once because of your birthmark?"

I pause to sip the tea the server had set down, giving her a chance to walk away. "Yes. It was my last life cycle." I pull up those memories as well as the dream. "I was six. My parents, Edward, and Evie had rented a beach house for a week. It was our third day there. Someone must have seen us and reported it to Felicia."

"That makes sense," he said as the server returns with our food. Just filling the silence. She does not need to know what we are discussing.

I take a fry and pop it into my mouth. I moan. "This is good." I eat another. "Anyways, we were returning to the house after swimming.

Edward had gone back to get drinks and snacks. Before he could return, Felicia and two of her minions came up to us."

I pause to eat some of my burger, savoring the moment. "The minions acted like they would leave us alone, then circled behind us. While Felicia distracted Evie, the goons grabbed me. Felicia stabbed Evie in the stomach, killing her slowly, but Evie still fought for me as best she could. Edward came out of the house, but the goon slit my throat before he could reach us."

I stop to catch my breath. The flood of memories make it feel as if it had happened yesterday, even though it was eighteen years ago.

We finish eating mostly in silence. "Since my memories returned, I've been looking for you," he said. I nod. That was always our pattern. "After a couple of years, I took a job for the regional training of big cats.

I did this because you have always been a cat of some sort. Every six months, I rotate regions, except East. I don't get along with Tony; I don't like how he treats his shifters."

Logical. With his position, he could travel to find me. "It just took longer for me to reach puberty." He nod.

Hunter pays for our meal, and we walk out hand in hand, climbing back on the bike to head south.

We arrive at Moody Gardens, a place with several pyramids. After paying the entrance fee, we join the line for the tour. The tour provided basic information before letting us explore on our own.

A group of about twenty people has gathered when a man in a Moody Gardens shirt with "Tour Guide" on the back joins us.

"Hello, everyone. My name is Tom. Welcome to Moody Gardens!" he greets loudly. "Moody Gardens began in 1983. When we opened, we were not what we are today." He pauses. "We started with just a horse barn, a riding area, and a writing program for people with head injuries, a dream to create an extraordinary island destination."

Walking, he continues, "Two years later, an eight-phase master plan was created. In 1986, the land you're standing on was secured for the hippo-therapy program." He pauses to indicate the area. "Later, we added animal and horticultural therapy for education, employment, and people with disabilities."

He stops to face us. "The same year, the Hope Arena..." He gestures to the building in front of him. "Opened." He resumes walking. I smile at Hunter; he knows I love places like this.

He continues the history. "In 1993, the rainforest area and the 3D theater opened, offering views of exotic plants and animals. The 3D theater was the first of its kind."

I want to run straight to the Rainforest pyramid. I squeezed Hunter's hand and bounce on the balls of my feet in excitement. He just smiles, love shining in his eyes.

The guide resumes, "In 1997, we opened our second pyramid, collaborating with NASA on space-inspired exhibits. In 1999, we opened the hotel and aquarium, featuring oceans worldwide. Our aquarium is among the largest globally." He concludes the tour with basic information and leaves us to explore.

As everyone disperses, I look at Hunter. Our eyes meet, and I smile. I am so excited I can not stand still. I walk backward, pulling him with me toward the rainforest. I do not ask where he wants to go; I know he has brought me here to explore, and I am determined to do exactly that.

For the next several hours, we explore each exhibit and watch a 3D movie. It is a fantastic date. I honestly couldn't think of anything better.

CHAPTER TWENTY-ONE

Cadence

A FTER THE LONGEST LUNCH date in history, we make our way back to the Farm. Most people are already in bed by this time. That does not bother me, though. I had the absolute best time.

Hunter walks me to my bedroom door. I thought for a moment he is coming in with me, but then he kisses me softly before saying goodnight and leaving me alone outside my bedroom door.

I make my way into my room, completely exhausted from the long day. I am asleep on my feet. I strip out of my clothes and leave them on the floor beside the bed.

Collapsing face down on the bed, I am asleep before my head even lands on the pillow. I lay in the bed sideways. I do not even take the time to lie down properly.

When I wake, the sun is shining through the window, turning the room into a whole new scene from the night before. I slowly sit up to give myself a chance to wake up fully, or close enough to it.

I pick my phone up and unplug the charger. I need to talk to my bestie. There is so much to update her on. I need to just hear her voice, but that didn't happen because she was still asleep, and no one answers the phone.

Since she didn't pick up, I call the second person on my list for the morning. "Hello, Cady-did." I hear my mother's voice.

"Good morning, Mom." I greet. "How did you know it was me?"

She laughs. "You are the only one that calls this early in the morning. That and the caller ID."

"How are things going down there?"

I flop back on the bed. "They are so good, Mom. I met this guy..."

She sighs loudly, interrupting me. "A boy? Cadence Ann Robinson, you did not go down there to start messing with boys. You went down there for three months to train and learn how to protect yourself."

I let her get it all out before I start again. "Mom, hang on, let me finish, please. This boy I met happens to be my fated mate. The one person that the Goddess gave me and only me a very long time ago."

It took a bit of convincing, and even me telling her about my memories, for her to understand just what Hunter meant to me. No one, not even her, would stand in between us.

After I end the call, I managed to dress and make my way down the stairs. My stomach is urging me on again. I have never been so hungry in my life until I became a shifter.

Stepping outside, I find my usual sight. All my new friends and Hunter are sitting at our table, chatting while they eat. Hunter was a friend as well, but he was also my fated mate.

I make my way over and sit down next to my mate. He smiles at me but turns back to Adam. I joined them as they were in mid-conversation.

"Hunter tells us we are all going to Houston today," Mack tells me as soon as I am seated.

I look up at her, confused. "Oh, you didn't know?" she turns to Hunter. "Did I ruin a surprise?"

I follow her gaze to him. He shakes his head. "No, I just planned it this morning," he chuckles. "Sleepyhead was still in bed," he turns to me. "I figured our friends could go with us today. You don't mind, do you?"

I hate it when he puts me on the spot. For this, I do not mind as much, but it's still annoying. I did or do enjoy hanging out with these guys. Even Travis is growing on me a little, once he got over his prejudice. I can see why the others hang out with him.

"You know I don't mind," I tell him the little white lie, then turn back to Mack. "When do we leave? I have to tell you guys about yesterday. It was so amazing." I say, trying to bring Anna into the conversation.

We finish our food while talking about the day before. The guys had gone back to whatever they were talking about before I had arrived.

When everyone was finished and our dishes put away, we make our way to a.., van. "This van belongs to the Farm," Hunter informs us. "I requested it to use this morning. This way we could take one vehicle instead of two."

Mack, Anna, and I climb into the far back seat while Travis takes the center, leaving Adam and Hunter to take the front. Hunter is driving, of course.

Headed north this time, we make our way to Houston, straight to the *Space Center*. After seeing the pyramids yesterday, it was kind of cool to go to the *Space Center* itself today. I kept finding myself comparing the two places to see what was the same.

Everywhere we went, Hunter and I were hand in hand. Stealing little looks and kisses as we could. We thought we were being discreet until we were caught. "Y'all look so cute together," Mack tells us as we make our way back to the van.

I just smile at her. I know she still has some feelings toward him, but I know she understands fated mates as well, even though she does not have all her memories yet. Maybe once her memories come in, she will find that she no longer feels the same about her friend.

Next, we make our way to the *Holocaust Museum*. This stop once again has a tour guide who tells us all about the place. He tells us all about the history of this historical attraction. He informs us it was built to honor the survivors and to remember the victims of the Holocaust.

"In 1981, a man named Siegi Izakson, a survivor of the Holocaust himself, realized that he and the other survivors were getting older. Some had already passed away. They were taking their knowledge of what had happened with them to the grave." He pauses to let that sink in.

"He decided to create an *Education* Center, which opened in 1996. With this *Education* Center, he could save the knowledge and the memories and share them with the world so they could never be forgotten."

The six of us make our way around the whole place, stopping to not only look at everything but to talk about each exhibit and our own experiences.

For shifters, most of us have seen firsthand what the Holocaust was, but we also value history. We have lived through it in one way or another. Even if we had died during the events. We still hold that knowledge. We can not share that with the public, though.

We would have a riot on our hands if the humans at large ever found out about us, but we had strict rules because of that. One of those rules was that we kept our knowledge to ourselves.

We make it back to the Farm by supper. More accurately, right before it is cleared away. We hurry to grab what was left and made our way to our table.

⁕

The next several days went almost the same. One day, Hunter and I would be alone. The next day we would go out with our friends.

The days Hunter and I would go by ourselves were romantic. There were walks on the beach, candlelit dinners, and such. Just being able to spend so much violence-free quality time with him was everything.

When our friends were with us, we would do more group-friendly outings, like walking around the zoo all day. I took it as a challenge to try to shift into each animal we came across. Unfortunately, it did not work that way. Which sucks. Turns out I cannot turn into the whole freaking zoo after all.

My mate sure got a laugh out of watching me try. We would have invited the others, but I am still mostly hiding what I am. I am doing well, so no one else had found out. I am also keeping my birthmark well covered.

To everyone but a select few, I am just Cadence, AKA Cady. The newbie shifter who just happened to be the granddaughter of the Central Region leaders. That shifts into a dog, a Search and Rescue animal. To the public, we as a group are just a bunch of teens like all the others out having fun. That's the way it needs to stay for now.

On the day of our anniversary, the day that Hunter and I met for the first time, so long ago, a week later, I wake to find a note on the pillow beside me, written in Hunter's beautiful handwriting.

"Happy anniversary, love. I leave this note as I have been called away. If it were something I could put off, I would have. I must go for now, since it is your safety that is at risk. I will, however, be back tonight. I will need you to meet me at a place in Galveston that is right near the ferry. Travis knows the location and has agreed to drive you there since he has a car.

See you at six.

Love,

Hunter."

I sigh and lie back down. I was looking forward to spending today, of all days, with my mate. I could count the number of anniversaries that we missed together on one hand and have fingers left.

On this date, many, many lifetimes ago, Hunter and I got married for the first time when we were brand new shifters. We had waited for a whole year to do so that we would have one anniversary date. Every day since our existence had begun has been about the other. Any lifetime that we are together on this date, we normally cannot be separated. Whatever the errand he had to do must have been important, or he would not have missed even a few hours of today.

CHAPTER TWENTY-TWO

Cadence

I GET UP AND make my way to the conference room. I need to check in with Granny anyway. It seems like forever since I talked to her, and we live under the same massive roof.

I make my way to the conference room only to find it empty. Well, not empty. The table is still there with all the chairs around it, but the desk is gone. The living room set that was along the back wall is also gone.

The room looks exactly like it did the first day I arrived here. Just a normal conference room. No extras. You couldn't even tell that this room had ever been used as an office.

How long had it been since I had been in this room? A week... Two... It could not have been longer than that.

As I stand there dumbfounded, a shifter that I have met once or twice walks up to me. His name was Carson or Carlton. Something like that.

He comes to a stop in front of me. "Is everything all right, dear?" he asks in that British accent of his.

"What happened?" I ask him but do not give him a chance to answer before I ask the next question. "Where did my grandmother go?"

He laughs lightly. "She went back to her office, dear. It was quite odd that she was using this space as it was." He pauses. I know he is trying to figure out what would cause her to change everything, even for a brief time. It was written all over his face. The confusion. The suspicion. The wonder.

I wonder what it would take for these people to start putting the pieces of this puzzle together.

The secrecy, the conference room, the extra security. I have seen them everywhere. So many more people here today than there were the day I arrived. Even if the conference room traveled back in time. The fact that every shifter and their uncle knew that the Black Dawn had been born.

Shaking my head slightly, I snap myself out of my thoughts. "Where is her office now?" I ask, drawing him out of his thoughts as well.

He looks up at me, startled. I guess he forgot where he was for a moment. "If you go back down this hall to the fireplace, you can take the hall on the other side. Her office is the first door on the left. You cannot miss it."

I smile and thank him before making my way in the direction he told me. When I reach the door he mentioned, there is a sign right there at eye level in gold. It has my grandmother's name and title on it. Even if Colin had not been so kind, I would have been able to find it with just a little exploring, if I knew where she was in the first place. Someone really should have told me she moved back to her office. Then again, if it had not taken me at least two weeks even to come see her, I would have known.

I knock lightly on the door. Shifter hearing as it was, I knew she would hear me. After a second, I opened the door and stepped in, and found all the missing furniture that had been in the conference room the last time; it was in there.

My grandmother is sitting at her desk, and the Beta female is sitting on the couch. That much has not changed, at least. The room itself was made of real wood paneling, making it look a bit rustic. There were picture frames on the wall behind her. Some of the people I had never met, but there was also a whole lot of me. Looks like my parents had sent her a lot of pictures over the years, and she hung them on her wall in her office.

"Hello, Cady." My granny says in greeting. "How are you?" At the same time, Emily says. "Hey, stranger."

I laugh at Emily. "Hello to you too." I turn back to my grandmother. "Hi, Granny. When did you move in here? I thought we needed the... benefits from the conference room?"

She nods and motions to the chair in front of her desk. "Have a seat, dear." I do as she asks. "A lot has changed since your memories came in." She looks over to Emily. She doesn't say anything, just gets up and closes the door. I had left it open.

Once the door was closed, Granny started again. "We have soundproofed this room. Well…" She pauses and tilts her head sideways slightly. "We have done a lot of things in the last two weeks. Do you know what a safe room is?" I guess she didn't hear the knock after all.

I nod. I do know what it is and why one would have such a room. "This office is now just that. It is completely sealed off from the outside. Even the Farm. If there was ever an issue that required that much, this room will protect you."

My grandmother and Emily went on to educate me on the entire room, all its functions, and how to use it properly. Once all the business was done, my grandmother smiled at me. "So please answer my first question." When I didn't answer right away, she reminded me. "How are you, honey?"

"Well…" I blush slightly. "…as you know, I found out that Hunter is my fated mate. That is amazing," I say, slightly embarrassed. This is still my grandmother. "Other than that, everything is going well. Business end, that is good as well. No sightings of Felicia on my end, even with us going out every day."

She nods. "Well, we are getting a few reports. Those things will have to be dealt with soon." She starts going through the files on the edge of her desk. When she finds the right one, she hands it to me.

I open the file folder to find several pages—missing flyers of sorts. Each page is a different shifter that is missing. It lists all the important details: the shifter's name, their stats, like date of birth in this life cycle, what region they are from, and where they were last seen. A normal missing persons flyer, but these had more details, like what they shifted into, for example.

I look up to meet my grandmother's eyes. "How far does this go back?" There were so many pages in the folder.

Sadness comes over her so strongly that I can feel it in the air. "That is just since you have been here."

I gasp. There must be close to fifty pages in this file folder that is still in my hands. "Why so many?" I ask, but I already know the answer to my own question. Felicia…it's always Felicia. "She must be planning something. Something big."

She nods. "There have never been so many missing in such a short time. The worst part is most have been found afterward. They show signs of being experimented on. Signs of torture." She hands me another file folder. I set the folder down that I was still holding to take this one. I almost didn't want to open it. I knew what I would find.

Taking a deep breath, I open the folder. Like ripping off a Band-Aid. Inside were photos. The people in the pictures were all dead. I could tell that instantly. The first few pictures looked like any other dead person. As I made my way through the stack, I could see what she meant. Some of the shifters were in half form, with odd limbs shifted into their animal form. Others were missing the same limbs. The rest are just mangled animals. So mangled that if we didn't know they were shifters, we would not be able to tell.

I look back at my grandmother with the same sadness and even horror on my face. "How could she do this to them? And why? It makes no sense." I close the folder with the pictures safely back inside. I can no longer look at them. "How is she even finding so many shifters?" The questions just keep coming.

Unfortunately, my grandmother or the beta female does not have the answers either. We sit and talk about all the things that could cause this sudden shift in Felicia. For longer than I have been a shifter, which has been a long time, Felicia would take about one shifter a month. There had been a time when she took more, but that time has passed. She knows that the longevity she seeks cannot be combined. By doing the spell too often, she will only reverse the effects of the spell in the first place.

Now she is doing experiments on them. What good would come from killing shifters without even taking their longevity? We may live longer than normal humans, but we are not immortal. The only reason we can come up with is that she could or would be doing this if she had found a new spell or a new way to gain something from our shifting abilities. She may even want to be a shifter herself, even though that is impossible. You are either born a shifter or you are not.

Chapter Twenty-Three

Cadence

WHEN THE TIME CAME to get ready for my anniversary dinner, I make my way back up the stairs to my room. If nothing else, these stairs should keep me in shape. I go up and down them so often that my legs don't even burn anymore. My body has completely adjusted.

I take my time getting ready. I want everything to be perfect. This is the first time in so long that we have been together on our actual anniversary. I take the extra time to blow-dry my hair and use heat curlers, making a soft wave in my normally super straight hair.

Even curled and pulled up halfway, my hair is still long enough to hang down past my ass—not quite knee length when it is styled this way. I apply my makeup carefully, then slip into a strapless black evening gown. The floor-length, shimmery material fits like a glove, highlighting the features I love so much about this body.

As I slip my feet into the sleek black heels that were bought to go with this dress, there is a knock on my bedroom door. "I hope you are decent," Anna calls as she lets herself into my room.

She stops as she takes in the sight of me. This is the first time I have worn anything so formal since I arrived here at The Farm. It has been at least four lifecycles since we were together the last time. Different bodies, same souls. Anna just stands there for so long with her mouth open that I wonder if her mouth starts to dry out.

I clear my throat to bring her attention to my face. "Sorry, you are beautiful. Hunter is going to flip." She laughs, pulling the hand off from behind her back that I didn't even notice was still behind her. In her hand, she held a single long-stemmed red rose. She holds it out to me. "Happy anniversary, by the way."

I take the rose from her, bringing it to my nose and inhaling the sweet fragrance. "Thank you." I turn to go into the bathroom to put the rose in water, but she stops me.

"Bring it with you." She smiles. "Just a bit of color. Travis is ready downstairs." She smiles, then turns to leave without saying any more. That is unlike her.

She leaves me alone, closing the door behind her. I quickly transfer my wallet and phone to a small clutch that matches my heels. I then go to the door. As I open the door, Emily is standing there with her hand raised to knock. She steps back. "Sorry about that," I tell her, because in my rush to get out the door, I almost ran her over.

She giggles and hands me a rose. "It's okay, I was just bringing this to you, and I wanted to let you know Rose sent me up here to ask you to come see her before you left." I take the rose with the same hand as the other one. Luckily, the thorns have been thoughtfully removed. "I see Anna beat me up here." She laughs again before turning and making her way back down the hall.

I just stand there for a moment, wondering what in the world is going on. Anna and Emily both have given me a red rose. Was this something that Hunter had planned? I do not know, but if I do not get moving, I will be late for our date, and that is not something I liked doing. I detest being late to anything.

I make way down to Granny's office without running into anyone else. When I enter the room, my grandmother is standing there holding yet another rose. "A rose for you. Happy anniversary, dear. You look amazing." She hands me the rose and leans in for a small hug.

"What is going on?" I ask her, looking down at the three roses in my hands. "First Anna and Emily, and now you."

She laughs. "You will have to ask your mate that question. We are just doing as he asked us to. Now go or you will be late."

Hunter is definitely up to something. I just shake my head and walk out the door right into my grandfather's arms. I stumble backwards, but he catches me by the arms before I can fall. Stupid heels. I should have worn shorter heels, but they weren't as pretty.

He holds on long enough for me to catch my balance, then releases me, adding yet another rose to my growing collection. "There you go," he says simply and just walks away. I shrug and follow.

As I am rounding the fireplace, Jameson is standing there with a smile on his face, and yet another rose in his hand. He hands me the rose without a word, then walks away. By now, I'm starting to get used to everyone I pass handing me roses. So, as I exit the first door, it is no surprise to see Mack and Adam standing on either side of the entryway. Each one was holding out a rose for me to take. I take them and add them to my collection. That makes seven. If a baker's dozen is thirteen, is seven half a baker's dozen?

I exit the last door only to find Travis standing beside a small red two-door Mazda holding out another rose for me. "Your chariot awaits." He smiles as I step into the car. He closes the door behind me, then heads to the driver's seat.

Travis is a good guy, but his nerdy ways sometimes showed through. He is definitely earning my trust back after he lost it all on that first disastrous day. I place the eight roses in my lap as we make our way to our destination. Wherever that was. Hunter didn't tell me much, just that my driver, who is also my friend, would take me.

We chat a bit, but the thirty-minute drive was over in no time. He pulls into the parking lot of a small restaurant. This place was not much bigger than Momma's. It is a lot different, too, though. It almost looked like Christmas had vomited on the exterior walls. Red paint, with green trim. It kind of looked like a Mexican restaurant. They could have picked different colors, though.

I take my clutch and my roses and step out of the car. I didn't take more than two steps before I was confronted with a very familiar face. Madi, my best friend from back home, was running right for me. In her hand, she held only a red rose. She barreled into me, not even giving me a chance to say a word.

"I missed you so much." She hugs me tight, then finally releases me. Holding me at arm's length, her gaze travels down my body. "Damn girl, the South is doing you good. You look great." She hands me the rose. "And that man of yours is so freaking smoking hot!"

I look up at her, stunned. "How are you here? You met Hunter?"

"I can't tell you anything." She mimes zipping her lips closed, then takes my hand and leads me towards the doors of the building. "There are more people who want to see you."

More people? Who else was here? I would have asked my questions, but as we crossed the threshold, I found myself wrapped in my mother's arms. She was squeezing me tight, just like the last time. The only difference was my skin was not super sensitive this time. My mother is tender-hearted. I loved her. I am her only child. She is allowed to get a little emotional at times.

My father came up behind me and wrapped both of us in a hug. My mother would not be letting up for a bit more. I knew it already. "What are y'all doing here?" I asked but got no answer.

Several minutes later, Madi cleared her throat. "Sorry to interrupt, but we need to take her inside," she told my parents.

My parents release me, handing me another rose each. That makes eleven. "It's good to see your kiddo, but you are needed in the next room," my father tells me. My mother just nods. She is extremely happy for some reason.

I step away from them, looking back one last time. I know my mate awaits me. That much I'm sure of. That and the fact that I would follow him anywhere life would take us. So, holding my roses in front of me, I hand my clutch to Madi, then turn to enter the next doorway.

As I step into the room, I see so many more roses, more than I have ever seen in one place in my life. They are everywhere. I was correct in thinking that this was a restaurant. All the decor was still scattered around the room. Now, though, there were roses mixed in. In the center of the room stood Hunter. He was holding one single rose in his hands.

I step closer, only seeing him, surrounded by all the red of the roses. Hunter is dressed in a black suit with a crisp white shirt underneath. His hair is slicked back. He holds out a hand for me to join him.

I step right up to him. I hear a commotion behind me, but I don't turn to look. The most important person is standing right in front of me.

"Every time we meet, in every new life cycle, you never fail to make me fall in love with you all over again. There has never been and will never be a lifetime that I didn't want to spend every second of my life with you as my wife." Hunter kneels down on one knee before me. "So, will you, Cadence Ann Robinson, do me the honor of agreeing to be my wife in this lifetime and all those that follow?"

I am already nodding. "Yes, so many times yes." I pull him up to me so that I can press my lips to his. This man is the love of my lifetimes. There will never be another; hopefully, we will be able to live this one to its fullest.

All of a sudden, there is clapping coming from behind me. So many people are clapping. I turn in Hunter's arms to find every single person who gave me a rose today. Eleven of my closest friends and family were standing in front of me.

Before I can do much more than glance, Hunter turns me back around to face him. He takes my left hand and slips a ring onto my finger. I don't even have to look at the ring;

I can already tell what ring it is just by the weight and feel of the warm metal against my skin. This is my ring—the very same ring he gave me the first time he married me, all those years ago.

I look down anyway. Seeing the beautiful silver wrapped around my finger once again brings tears to my own eyes. "How?" I gasp. "I thought this was lost forever."

He wipes the tears from my face. "I thought so too." He tells me. "I just happened to stumble across an estate sale. This ring and a few other interesting items were found there."

I did not really care where he found it. What I cared about was that I had my ring back. This ring was just as old as our love story. It will go on just as long, too, if I have any say in the matter.

Just then, we are interrupted by the servers of the restaurant coming through the swinging doors behind Hunter. There were about fifteen of them, each carrying something different. They laid the dishes on the one table in the room that was free of roses. It looks like several tables had been pushed together to make room for all of us.

They laid everything out buffet style in the center of the tables, setting glasses of ice down in front of each chair. "Congratulations on the nuptials," said one of the men with a Spanish accent. "Please enjoy your meal, and if you need anything at all, please don't hesitate to ask."

We all took our places at the table. We ate and drank and laughed for hours. Hunter had actually rented the entire place out for the whole day. Which was very romantic if you ask me. Once we were all finished eating, my grandparents allowed my parents to follow us back to The Farm. For the first time since the Central Region set up shop on that property, they were allowing a human to enter. Two, if you count my dad as a human.

Unfortunately, Madi had to stay at a motel with her parents. They didn't mind or did not say anything about it. We would all be leaving first thing in the morning, headed right back to Missouri. It had not been a fun conversation to have with my mother. There were tears...again. I think, by the end, she understood a little better, but was still not happy.

The problem, however, was the shifters back at the Farm. When the car, which Hunter had borrowed, pulled up to the house, we could see a small group of people standing right in front of the door. Well, two groups: one was a small group of shifters that I didn't recognize, and the other included my grandparents and my parents. My grandparents stood about halfway between.

"What is going on here?" Hunter asks. We both step out of the car at the same time. We rush forward right at the man in front of the group who speaks. I can tell this is something he is repeating by the tone of his voice. "It doesn't matter. A human is not allowed to be here. They do not belong here at all."

I automatically knew what he was talking about now, or rather, whom. My parents. I push my way in front of them. No one was going to get through me. "You don't get a say in this, Dallas," my grandfather tells the man. "Unless this is a challenge to our authority?" Both my grandparents take another step closer to the group in front of us, one step further away from the two humans.

Dallas appeared to be thinking about this. Was he honestly thinking about taking on both my grandparents at the same time just to keep a couple of humans—humans who already knew all about our kind—off the property?

I would not let this happen. I lift my foot to take a step closer to the group in front of me, only for my grandmother's gaze to snap to mine. She jerks her head so fast it's almost comical, but the look on her face is not. I have never had this type of look directed at me, especially not from my own grandmother.

There was authority there, anger, and even a clear order, all combined into one single look. It startles me so much that instead of stepping forward, I actually step back.

The queen of all shifters. Grandmother or not, Rose Robinson does not have the authority to order me to do anything. I simply outrank her.

I think she realizes this at the same time I do, because the fierce look she had before changed so fast that if I wasn't looking directly at her, I would be second-guessing myself. She is no longer the Central Region leader; she is no longer showing any hostility whatsoever. She was back to just being my grandmother.

However, the damage is already done. A part of me would always remember this. Even if she is my own flesh and blood in this lifetime.

The whole incident between Rose and me couldn't have lasted longer than a minute. Even if it felt like it had gone on forever, Dallas cleared his throat, bringing both of our attention back to what was going on in front of us.

"No. That is not a challenge. I would never challenge either of you." He bows slightly, tilting his head to the side. All the men behind him do the same, even though a couple hesitate. I remember their faces. Maybe those people are the reason Rose stopped me from doing what I planned. Maybe she knew they would back down, and we are not completely surrounded by those she trusts.

Rose must have known he was not a real threat. You would think that if she did think there was a possibility, she wouldn't have taken her attention away from the situation at hand. She would never have, in a way, challenged my own authority. Even if she was trying to warn me not to step in, she should have found another way.

My grandfather nods at Dallas. "Then move aside."

The six men standing before us, blocking the entrance of the house, moved at once. They didn't say another word as we all made our way past them. Hunter is on one side of my parents, and I am on the other.

CHAPTER TWENTY-FOUR

Cadence

T HE DRIVE BACK TO my childhood home was a lot different from leaving it. For one thing, I was not passed out in the back seat for the entire trip. Second, Hunter is sitting on my left side, and Madi is on my right. My parents are doing the driving.

This time it was fun. Just like one of the road trips that we used to take when I was younger. This one was way better, though, because of the two people sitting next to me. They make all the difference.

As we passed the Cape City limits sign that evening, I felt the sadness come over me. It was saddening to see this trip come to an end. Soon, I would have to say goodbye once again to three of my favorite people.

Hunter and I are staying a couple of days, though, because tomorrow is Madi's eighteenth birthday. I would not miss that for anything in the world.

We drop off Madi with her parents. They are already home. I guess they did not stop at as many places as we did. We had stopped at several of the tourist attractions along the way, just staying long enough to use the restroom, grab snacks, and hit the road again.

We said our goodbyes, then made our way to our parents' house, the home I grew up in. And looking at it through the eyes of a stranger, especially after spending so much time at the Farm, I am grateful for my parents giving me the normal life they did.

The two thousand eight hundred square foot, four-bedroom, three-bath home that sits at the edge of town was perfect for growing up in.

The front door opens to an open area. That area housed the living area, the kitchen, and the dining area, as well as the stairs that led up to the second floor. Three doors lead to other parts of the lower level: my parents' bedroom, the guest room, and the last door to the mudroom, washroom, and the guest bathroom.

The upstairs area is where my room is. There is also another bedroom and a bathroom up there.

As we walk through the front entry, I am hit with the smell of cinnamon mixed with something else, maybe sticky buns. The scent is faint because my parents have not been home, but it is still there. The smell of home.

Growing up here, there was always something mixed with cinnamon going in the wax burner. That is my mother's favorite smell. Every once in a while, she would try something else, but she always came back to the old faithful.

I stop just inside the door to close my eyes and take the familiar scent deep into my body. I am home. Nothing could change the fact that this smell would always remind me of home.

Hunter stops behind me, giving me the space I need. He doesn't stop me. He doesn't say anything. After a few heartbeats, I open my eyes and step out of his way so that he can fully come into the house.

I make my way toward the stairs, calling over my shoulder to my parents, "Good night." I make my way to my room with Hunter on my tail. I look over at him to make sure he is following. He is.

This is the first night, in this lifetime, that Hunter will be staying with me. The full night. The other day in his bed does not count as it wasn't night. We are both exhausted and in my parents' house. So, unfortunately, there will be nothing going on but sleeping.

"Here we are," I tell him as I open my bedroom door and step to the side to let him go in first. He is carrying both of our bags.

He sets the bags down just inside the door and looks around, taking in the full-size bed in the corner, as well as the desk and vanity that belonged to my mother's mother. Of course, there are posters all over the walls as well.

There are animals everywhere.

As I take in my room, I begin to wonder if I knew in my heart that I was really a shifter. Because looking at my décor, I can see it as clear as day. Everywhere I look, I am seeing one form of myself or another staring right back at me.

The bedspread itself was a custom print that my parents had ordered for me for my fifteenth birthday. It has a jungle background; the focal point, though, is a dark tiger and a black panther curled up together. You can clearly see that they are lovers just by the way they look at each other.

I remember dreaming about this scene right before my birthday that year. I absolutely had to have the image of the two cats in real life. It took over a month of planning to get the image just right.

The posters on the walls are all different types of animals. I have all the different types of animals that I have always loved: tigers and lions, wolves and dogs.

Hunter turns to me with a smile. "Everything about this room screams ... you." He laughs softly. He takes me into his arms and presses a light kiss on my lips. He lifts his head all too soon, and his eyes go behind my head. "Is that the bathroom?"

I nod. He picks his bag up from the floor and heads into the bathroom to get ready for bed. While he is gone, I turn back the blankets and get my own pajamas out of the dresser, not bothering with the bag. When he comes out of the bathroom, we swap places. I head in to get myself ready for bed.

When I step back into the room, I find Hunter lying on the bed, on his side, in nothing but his bottoms. He is on top of the blankets, displaying all of those glorious muscles, just for me. Always for me.

I know that he is only in the pajamas because of where we are. He hates sleeping in pants. He always has. If we were alone, he would be wearing either his boxer shorts or nothing at all. Hunter has a lot of respect for my parents; that is the only reason he is still wearing his clothes.

He stands as I come in, so I climb into bed and slide over close to the wall. Hunter climbs in after me. After getting the blanket settled. I snuggle in next to him, wrapping my arms around his waist. He leans down and places a soft kiss on the top of my head. "Good night, Cadence," he whispers to me. "I love you, sweetheart." This man melts my heart.

The next thing I know is that I am opening my eyes to find a room full of light. I don't think I have moved once all night. I am still snuggled up close to Hunter with his arms wrapped around me.

His body is pressed up tight against me. The only difference is his rock-hard erection. It is pressed up against my thigh. I can feel the heat of him through my own clothes and his. His body is straining to reach me, even while he sleeps.

I slide my hand that is around his waist slowly down his body. I look up to make sure he is still sleeping, then slip my hands into the waistband of his pajama pants. As my fist wraps around his length, his eyes snap open. He groans softly but must remember where we are because his hand comes down to still mine. "We can't, baby," he tells me.

Groaning, I removed my hand from what I want most at this moment. Instead, I snaked my hands up around his neck and pressed a tight kiss to his lips. What started as innocent quickly turned into passion and heat. Just the way I like it.

After a moment, I pull back. "If you really want to stop, we might want to get up, because I am about two seconds from mounting you like a bull."

He smirks. "You know I want the same thing, my love, but we need to wait until we get back to the Farm." He kisses my nose to soften the rejection. "Just a couple more days." He slides off the bed. I just lay there watching how his muscles flex and move. He is on the way out the door.

I flop back on the bed. "Ugh." I guess I need to get up. I slowly make my way over to my closet. I open the double doors and just stare into the space. I have two days to pack all of this—well, what I plan to take with me back to the Farm anyway.

For now, all I want to do is shower and go find some food. I grab a set of clothes and close the doors just as Hunter walks back in. He is freshly showered and wearing a clean set of clothes. The fragrance of his body wash filled the room ahead of him. I cannot wait to get home.

Hand in hand, we make our way down the stairs. The smell of bacon filled the air, and I led the way. My stomach makes a noise right then to show its pleasure. I laugh. "Good timing," Hunter whispers.

CHAPTER TWENTY-FIVE

Hunter

CADENCE AND I MAKE our way into the kitchen, where Carol is just finishing up breakfast. "Good morning," she calls over her shoulder as she loads two plates with food.

"Morning," I say at the same time Cadence says, "Good morning, Mom."

We sit at the bar as Carol places the plates in front of us. "What would you like to drink?" she asked me. There is already a glass of milk in front of Cadence.

She opens the refrigerator to show me that she has several options. "Coffee?" I ask. I look around for a coffee pot. I know there must be one because she has a cup herself.

She hands me a cup. I refuse any add-ins, though. I enjoyed my coffee black—most of the time anyway.

"What do you two have planned for today?" she asks.

I just look at Cadence. I am shadowing her today. I know we are doing a few things around here and then going to end up at her friend's party, but other than that, I am not sure.

Cadence swallows the bite of food she has in her mouth. "I am going to pack. Then Madi's party is later. That's about it," she tells her. I was correct.

"I guess you don't need my help for any of that," she chuckles. "It's a good thing. I will be out most of the day." She apparently has a few appointments that were set up before she knew we were coming.

Cadence nods. "No problem, Mom. We got this," she laughs.

Carol is true to her word; not even an hour later, we hear her leave the house. We have made our way back upstairs with a few boxes to pack up Cadence's belongings to move to the Farm permanently. At least semi-permanently for now.

All she has really managed to do so far is make a mess. There are clothes everywhere. On the bed, the desk, and even the floor. I have taken two boxes to her car for her.

Cadence stops in the middle of the room with her hands on her hips. She just looks around at the mess that she has made. "I think we are about done," she sighs. I know this is a big, surreal moment for her. "I just need to clean up now."

That is a bit of an understatement. I laugh. The room is a whirlwind of chaos. She bends over to pick up a stray shirt off the floor. Her beautiful green eyes sparkle with amusement.

When she straightens up, she tosses the shirt right at my head. She giggles, then finds another and does the same.

I rush her before she can throw a third. I tackle her playfully to the ground right on top of a pile of clothes to be donated, and I tickle her sides—anywhere I can reach.

She laughs so hard. We had been so busy training that we hadn't had much time for just fun and play. We need to make sure to make more time for just fun. Just to be with each other.

"Enough!" she squeals. I stopped tickling her, but do not move away. We are so close that we are sharing the same breaths. The air crackles with a spark of electricity that is flowing between the two of us. And a love that will never fade.

The room, the mess, and even our world—all that falls away in this moment. This is just the two of us. I close the scant distance and take her mouth in a searing kiss.

As we kiss, I let my hands roam all over her body, not able to get enough when it comes to the love of my lifetime. I slipped my hand under her top to cup the weight of her breast in my hand.

As I tweak her nipples with my fingers, she lets out a gasp that I quickly swallow up with my mouth. I can hear every thump of her heart, and I am sure mine is just as erratic.

In the next moment, nothing else mattered but going home. It didn't matter where they were or even if somebody tried to walk in at that moment. Nothing would stop me. I had to be inside her now.

Releasing my claws, I sliced through Cadence's shirt and bra in one go. I would buy her more if needed. I needed to get to her bare flesh, and I need it now.

Breaking the kiss, I bring my mouth down to the now exposed breast. I take her nipple into my mouth as I pinch the other between my thumb and finger, giving just enough pressure to make her moan. She has always been responsive to my touch, and I marvel at the sounds she makes just for me.

Moving from one nipple to the other, I take my now free hand and move it down her side and over her hip, taking her pants and lacy underwear with me. I quickly discard my own clothing before taking her mouth in another heated kiss.

"Wrap your legs around me, baby." I lean up and take my cock in my hand. I want to watch as my cock disappears inside of her. I rest the crown right at her entrance, but don't move to enter her yet. I just savor the moment.

Cadence attempts to impale herself on me, but I hold her still. Her breath hisses out in a whimper, as if she wants me to fuck her just as badly as I do.

My cock throbs as a bead of precum leaks out. I slide in just a little; I need her to adjust to my size. She is so fucking tight. I slide in just a bit more. Her body is giving way to mine.

"Hunter, please fuck me. Now!" she begs. I slowly worked my way into her tight heat. When I am fully seated, I pull back slowly almost all the way out, and just pause again. I look into her beautiful green eyes as I plunge back in. Her eyes flutter, and the most beautiful sound escapes her lips.

Her arousal coats my cock, making the next thrust go in just a bit easier. A little bit deeper.

"You are so tight, baby, but also very wet." I thrust into her again. "Made just for me." I run my nose along her neck. She always smells so good. My mouth finds hers again as I pick up my pace, letting her have me just the way she likes. I rock my hips, setting a perfect pace, making sure to hit her G-spot deep inside. Her legs and her breath are growing faster as her inner walls clamp down on me. "That's it, baby," I croon as I break our kiss. She pants for air. "Come for me, baby." I thrust harder. "I want to feel you come on my cock. Give it to me."

Her eyes rolled back in her head as she let go. "Good girl."

Her skin is flushed and damp with perspiration. Her legs are trembling, then her walls start to tremble, squeezing my cock like it never wants to let go. I drive into her once, twice, and follow her into oblivion.

CHAPTER TWENTY-SIX

Cadence

THE JUNE HEAT IN Missouri is miserable. The humidity instantly makes us sweat, making our clothes stick to our bodies in seconds. Even at six in the evening, the temperature is still ninety degrees, with the humidity over seventy percent.

Still buzzing from my post-orgasmic glow, or maybe because of it, this day has already been amazing. I figured today would be yet another bittersweet moment in an ever-growing list of them, but I cannot help but be thrilled.

Since getting my memories from my past lives, I am even more galvanized. I have lived and died so many lifetimes because of what evil will or will not do to end my happiness. I am done with that.

I am going to make the most of every moment I get. Even if it's just cleaning up a mess I made and having an impromptu romp in said mess. I must take the time to have and enjoy those little moments because those little things are what is most important in life.

It's the little things that make all the difference. It's what makes a life worth living, no matter how short it is.

That includes walking hand in hand with the love of my lifetimes in the Missouri heat wave. We are currently headed to Madi's birthday party. I will be able to spend one more evening with my best friend before moving away on a more permanent basis. The best part, though, is that I get to include Hunter in the festivities.

I am so exhilarated. I bounce on the heels of my flip-flops as I clutch Hunter's hand. "I cannot wait to introduce you to all of my friends!" I pause to think. "I wonder who all is still in town."

Hunter gives me a heartwarming smile. I can tell he is a little uncomfortable, but he would do anything for me, even risk his own life for mine... he has done so before. That goes both ways. I would do the same for him in a heartbeat. That's how true fated mates work.

"How long are we going to be there?" he asks me.

I look up at him. "Normally, we girls, about ten of us, would end up turning the party into a slumber party." He groans. "Hang on, baby. That is not happening this year." I am quick to add.

He lets out a sigh of relief.

"This year...the party will only last a few hours. There will be pizza, fun games, and even a dance-off."

As we approach Madi's house, we can tell the party is already in full swing. We can hear music and laughter coming from the backyard.

I push my way into the front door without knocking. This house has always been like a second home to me. Mine is the same way for Madi.

We walk into organized chaos. The normally clean, elegant lines of Madi's living room are now covered in streamers, balloons, and tables that were not there the last time I was there. One of the tables is overflowing with snacks of all kinds, including pizza and drinks. The other table is full of presents for the birthday girl.

The room is empty of occupants, so we make our way through the living room and kitchen to the back door that will lead to the backyard and the pool.

Since Madi was about ten, every year we started in the pool before coming in to do the food and cake. We would play all the games in the pool itself and then finish the night off with a dance-off.

As we exit the back door of the house, Madi jumps out of the pool and runs straight toward us. She wraps her wet, bikini-clad body around me. "Happy birthday, bestie," I tell her with a laugh.

"Thank you for coming. It would not be a celebration without my bestie," she says as she pulls back. She moves to hug Hunter, not quite as enthusiastically.

"Happy birthday, Madison," he tells her.

Most people in a situation like this might be a little jealous. A half-naked, beautiful woman is wrapped around your fiancée, but I know how Hunter feels about me. I am completely confident in him—no doubts whatsoever.

As far as Madi, I know for a fact she would never cross that line and risk our relationship. We are too important to each other. Another thing, I have a sneaky suspicion I know exactly what the reason is for Madi's parents only allowing a few hours for her party this year.

Madi laughs, bringing my attention back to her. "No, sir," she tells Hunter. "Call me Madi. You are marrying my best friend. You cannot full-name me." She turns back to the pool behind her, where several of our friends from high school are playing and swimming. "Now let's go swim," she says as she walks back off toward the pool. When she gets there, she jumps straight off into the deep end, hollering, "cannonball!"

I glance up at Hunter, who shrugs and reaches behind him to grab the collar of his shirt. I am momentarily stunned into silence, staring at his Adonis belt. I am one lucky girl. Heat settles low in my belly. It has nothing to do with the weather.

I smile at his raised eyebrow. He knows what I am thinking. He knows me too well. I know we can't do anything about that, though. So, I just removed my cover-up.

"Hey, Cady," is the first thing I hear as we make our way slowly into the pool. No cannonball for us. Not yet anyway.

"Hey, guys," I tell them, then turn back to look at Hunter. He is standing right behind me, but not touching me. "This here is my fiancée, Hunter." I turned back to face the others and back right into my mate's waiting arms.

"This is Emily and Ethan." I point to the only other couple in the pool. Then I point to the others as I go. "Eric, Savannah, Erica, Pete, and Donnie." They all greet Hunter.

"Now that introductions are out of the way... who wants to play a game?" Madi asks us.

We end up playing several games, some more than once. We play for two hours before Kim, Madi's mother, asks us all to dry off and head inside.

Once we are situated in the cluttered living room, Kim sets up the candle on the cake, while Madi's dad hands out pizza and drinks. Once the candles are lit, everyone starts to sing. "Happy birthday to you, happy birthday to you..."

Madi blows out her candles, but before she can even move back, her mom snickers and pushes the cake right into her face, getting the extra gooey icing everywhere. "I couldn't pass up on that opportunity," Kim says as everyone laughs.

Madi then decides to share her cake icing with everyone who laughed. She chased each and every one of us around the room until everyone had at least a little on their faces or in their hair. "That's what you all get for laughing at me." We laugh again.

Kim then goes to the kitchen and brings back an even bigger cake than the one she pushed in her daughter's face. "We will eat this one." She tells us, then starts to cut it. After we all finished the cake and ate our food, Madi started in on the pile of presents. I kept catching her parents looking up at the clock. This made me look up as well. It was really close to nine at night.

I look over at Hunter, sitting beside me. "*Are you thinking what I'm thinking?*" I asked him telepathically. His face jerks towards me, but he stays silent. I don't think he remembered that I could do this in any form.

Since I am opening the path between the two of us, he can respond. If it wasn't for that he would not be able to speak to me like this unless he was in animal form. "*As close as they are watching the clock I'm sure everyone knows that they are up to something. Only the two of us probably know the real reason though.*"

I nod and Kim catches my movement, but she has no idea who I am and what I can do so she just goes back to watching Madi and the others. "*Do you think they will be pissed if we follow them?*"

"*Most definitely.*" He tells me. "*How will we follow them though?*"

I stop to think about this. We cannot shift in the middle of town. Well... I can but he cannot. I can use the Newfoundland, but he only has the tiger. That big of a cat in this town where we don't even have a zoo with do nothing but draw unwanted attention. We will have no choice but to take the car, but at that time of night it will still be risky. "We have no choice but to take the car, at least most of the way."

Right as the clock hits nine, Kim tells everyone that we have to leave. She is always nice, but she did rapidly end the party. Everyone including Hunter and I are out of the house with in fifteen minutes.

On our way out the door, I put a little round happy birthday sticker that was inside on the taillight of Kim's car. I am hoping that is the one they take. If they take her father's car it won't work.

"Great idea. It will be easier to tell which car is theirs in the dark." Hunter tells me as we make our way back down the block.

We stop at the house long enough to change out of our wet clothes then head out to the car. Hunter is driving, so I slip into the passenger seat. He pulls out and goes around the block once and parks on the side of the road. There are so many here that it would be easier to blend in.

Less than an hour later, the three of them come out of the house and luckily pick Kim's car. I figured they would because normally when they go anywhere as a family they take her car.

As they round the first corner, Hunter pulls out behind them. With the sticker on the back end of the car we can easily see which one is theirs. We did lose them once but found them again a few blocks up the road. They were headed to the interstate, and we only found them because I know this area. Growing up here, helped me learn all the back roads.

They hit the interstate headed south. They took the Benton exit and turned right. This smaller town did not do us any favors in staying hidden. We ended up having to pull off at the dollar store and wait for them to get over the hill before getting back behind them.

Finally, about fifteen minutes later, they pull off the main road. Headed off into a strand of trees. We go on past them and end up parking the car at the edge of a corn field. The car would be hidden enough here. We then take off on foot.

The night envelopes us as soon as we step out of the car. It does not take long to find them again. Thanks to all that running Hunter has made me do recently. They are standing in the center of a clearing. It is different from where I had my moonlight ceremony. Here there is no creek. No pretty sights. Nothing but a clear patch of tall grass surrounded by tall trees.

Madison is standing facing her parents, as they talk to her. My bestie is not happy. I'm sure she is feeling a lot of what I was feeling, but it makes me wonder, since she had two shifter parents, if they prepared her any better before tonight than I was.

Before long, her parents step back, leaving Madison in the center of the clearing by herself. I already know she is going to shift. What I don't know is what she will shift into this time.

With only a few minutes to spare, I notice movement on the far side of the clearing. It takes me a moment to realize that it is not an animal. I nudge Hunter and he nods. He sees the movement as well. Then, as if they belong here, three people step out of the trees, headed right for my best friend.

CHAPTER TWENTY-SEVEN

Hunter

CADENCE AND I EXCHANGE a look. We do not need to speak. We are in agreement here. That one look told us all we needed to know about what the other was thinking. We will break our own rules to save the Millers, no matter the consequences. We will do it side by side, like we always have.

We step out of the tree line as one. I think I see Cadence's hands start to shake just slightly, but she presses them tight against her thigh too quickly for anyone but me to notice. Every single person in the field turns as we do. All of their gazes snap to us in a heartbeat. That does not stop us, though. We continue to walk toward the two groups, only stopping once we are standing between the two groups of three.

One friend.

One foe.

The elder Millers take up defensive stances in front of their daughter, like any good parent would do, blocking even the view from the newcomers. As we come to a stop, I can see exactly what we are up against: witches. It's always witches. The three of them stop their forward movement as we step between them and the Miller trio.

"What are you doing here, Cady?" Kim asks. There is a bite of reprimand but also fear. The fear is masked by the reprimand, but I can still sense that it is there. I can see the fear for their daughter in both of the elder Millers' faces.

Cadence does not respond to Kim aloud. I can tell by the tilt of my mate's head that she is answering her telepathically.

Simultaneously, she took up the fighting stance that I taught her. I step up next to her and do the same. "What business do you have here?" she asks the witches. There are two males and one female.

The one in the middle, who looked like the leader of the group, took one step closer to us. "This is none of your concern, child," he said with a sneer. "But five instead of three will bring us a big prize." The sneer turns to glee as the three of them reach into their shoulder bags, as if it were a practiced move.

"Oh, he is going to be so happy we got five of them," the female whispers. If it were not for our advanced hearing, I wouldn't have heard her.

I know Cadence has their attention for the moment, so I turn to look behind me. Madison has fallen to the ground, and her shift has begun. They cannot move. They are trapped right where they are. "We will take care of the witches; you protect Madi," I tell them. I turn back to face the actual threat in front of us. I notice that the two witches who are still in the back are slowly moving their hands around in their bags. I can hear a faint chant.

"You have one chance to turn around and leave, three seconds to make your decision, but I guarantee you will not get to the shifters behind me," Cadence issues the warning, then adds.,"Nor us."

They laugh at her. Big mistake. Cady hates to be laughed at. Always has. "What are you going to do, little girl? You cannot stop us."

Cady nods, taking that as their answer. The three of them reach into the messenger bags they have. Each pulls out little vials, but before they can even do anything with them, the so-called little girl is no longer standing before them. In her place is a glorious beast.

I have seen the panther many times over the last few weeks, but it has also changed.

Just looking at her now makes her look like a large cat straight from Hell. She still has the soot-black fur with the faint charcoal-grey rosettes, which are almost undetectable in the moonlight. The sleek, muscular body now holds a light of its own. The beast's paws are now shrouded in faint flames, as if someone had lit them aflame.

All of the hesitation she held before is completely gone. Now in her place stands a regal, dauntless being, one who is completely confident in her ability to save her best friend.

The witches freeze, right there in the middle of the clearing. Hands raised but no longer moving. They just stared at the flames that I know shimmered in her eyes. "What..." The first one squeaked out. Cadence didn't even give them a chance to turn. There would be no running today.

The muscular body of the cat leaped into the air. It landed gracefully on the chest of the leader. She was not looking at that one, though. Her eyes were on the other two; she swiped out with her flaming paws, slicing and cauterizing the wounds of the witch on the right. The smell of burnt flesh filled the air.

The third then attempted to turn and run, but I was standing right behind him. I cannot shift as fast as Cadence, so I resorted to using my claws, which I can change in an instant. I held those claws right at his throat and herded him right back to my mate. As the witch in my grasp turned back to face Cadence, the beast bent down and chomped right into the witch's head, which was still under her flaming paws. The crunch was nothing like I had ever heard.

She released the head with a little shake before pouncing on the other remaining witch. He was on the ground holding his stomach. The one in my arms started to struggle. I think he would rather die by my claws than be eaten by my lovely mate. However, I didn't let him loose. I retracted my claws and just held him in place to watch as Cadence finished off his friend.

When she turned back to face the one in front of me, I started to smell urine. The witch that had come here to face down three shifters on one of said shifters' moons had just pissed his pants.

"*Eww, that's disgusting,*" Cadence tells me. "*But maybe this will show them.*" She tilted her head and stared at the witch.

Still in Hell Cat form, Cadence's voice rang through my head. "*I will let you live.*" She told the witch, but I could tell that I was not the only one hearing her words. Every living being in the clearing heard her loud and clear.

"*You will go back to Felicia, and you will tell her I am coming for her. Her days of destruction are over, but I have a parting gift for you first.*" She swipes out with her paws, once, twice, and a third time. The first was across his face, the second across his ribs, and the third took off his arm that had tried to throw the potion at her best friend. "*Release him, baby. Let him go.*" I do as she ordered. The witch, now crying uncontrollably, turned and stumbled from the clearing.

CHAPTER TWENTY-EIGHT

Cadence

I WATCH AS THE witch limps away. I can still hear the sounds of his whimpers of pain long after he is out of sight. Once I know for a fact that he or any others will not be coming back, I sag. Mentally only. There is no way I will allow myself to falter. There is still plenty to be done this night.

Glancing down to look at my paws. I saw the flames before, but I couldn't stop to look at them. I could not focus on anything but the threat that was here to kill my best friend. Looking at my paws now, though, you never would have known that they were on fire not five minutes before.

Now my paws are back to normal. Just my regular panther paws. I don't know where the fire came from or where it went. So, I don't think I would be able to bring it back. The flames were useful during the battle, and it would be a good skill to master. Since this has never happened before, this is all new to me.

A hand on my back brings me out of my thoughts. I look up standing beside me, I am almost chest high to him in this form. "Are you alright?" he whispers so only I will hear him.

Once again, I pause to evaluate myself. Physically, I think I am okay. The first witch I encountered did get a couple of hits on me while I was taking out his friend. I think he even hit me with a potion that was already in his hands, breaking the glass on my body. However, I don't believe anything is serious. There is glass embedded between my ribs from the glass vial. I will have to deal with that once we are gone from here.

Mentally, it might be another story. I killed two people tonight. Yes, I was protecting my loved ones, and in that moment, or any other, I wouldn't have cared how many I had to kill. Every single time, I will protect those people that I care about.

So yes, if I had to do it all over again, I would do it. I knew the two bodies were right behind me, but I really do not want to turn and look, even though I know I must do so eventually. But I have something else I must do first.

I rub the length of my body against Hunter as I turn around, just to show him without words that I am fine. I turn the opposite way from the bodies to face the Millers. From where I am, I cannot see much of Madi, but both Kim and Dale are standing tall, blocking Madi from anything that could try to sneak up on them.

I know that if I shift back to human, I will be at a disadvantage—the disadvantage of being naked. So, I stay as I am; they have already seen this form. I make my way to them. I stop a respectable distance away from Madi, who I can see now is still in the middle of her shift. She is almost finished, though.

"Hello, Mr. and Mrs. Miller," I tell them telepathically. I see the shock cross both of their faces. *"I am truly sorry for following you here. I know you sent me home. I swear I was only thinking about your safety and the safety of Madi."*

Kim steps one step closer to me. "How?" she asks.

I am not sure what she means. There are so many options: the form, the telepathy with them in human form, the flames. *"Madison and I have been friends in more than one lifetime. I have my memories. Well... most of them. Some things are a little fuzzy."* I don't think I need to answer any of the other possibilities. They see the panther in front of them. They would expect that, with being who I am, it would come with some differences from normal shifters.

As if she were reading my mind, Kim says, "You...You are the Black Dawn." She makes sure to make it known that she is using my title. I nod in answer as Hunter comes back to my side.

I rub against him again. He sinks his fingers into my fur, momentarily distracting me. The feel of his touch makes me want to rub more of my body against his.

"How often has this happened? Are you getting attacked like this often?" Hunter asks, looking over his shoulder at what I still don't want to face.

Dale steps up next to his wife. "This is the first time this has happened in our area, that I know about, but I have heard some rumors."

"What rumors?" I asked.

Kim is the one who answers. "A few area leaders are saying that moonlight ceremonies all over their areas are being invaded, and they are getting attacked." She pauses to look back at her daughter, who is still changing. There is almost a complete brown bear, but I can tell that she still has human parts. Why is it taking so long? "The shifters present at the moonlight ceremonies are being captured or killed on sight, if they fight back."

I wonder if that is what they were discussing at the last Summit meeting with the missing shifters, or even the photos that Granny had shown me just a couple of days ago.

"*We cannot let this continue...*" I tell Hunter.

"We will figure out what's happening, love. As soon as we get back to the Farm." He rubs his hand down my back. "We will fix this."

"*Who is the leader for this area now?*" I ask the Millers.

"Sofia and Theodore," she tells me, motioning to her and Dale. "We are their betas."

A sound draws my attention back to my friend. It seems she is nearing the completion of her shift. "*Please have them get in contact with Rose and Robert as soon as possible.*" I look up at Hunter.

"We are going to give you some privacy to be with your family." He looks over his shoulder at the mess we left back there. "Do you need us to take care of this? Or do the leaders of this area have cleaners?"

In answer to his question, Dale pulls out his cell phone and calls someone. "Hey Henry, we have a little issue that we could use your assistance with." He gives him the location and hangs up. "Henry is good at what he does. He will be here in fifteen minutes."

"*Good.*" I pause, almost forgetting the most important thing. "*You cannot tell anyone who I am.*" I shift into my tiger. Sliding from one animal to another is sometimes easier than the initial shift. "*This is safer.*"

Kim steps forward cautiously. "You are like another daughter to us." Hunter steps back as she wraps her arms around my neck. "We would never do anything to risk your safety."

"You don't have to worry about us, Cady, and thank you so much for following us. Without you here, we would have lost our baby." Dale turns back to glance at his daughter once more. I swear I saw a sheen in his eyes, but I would never point it out.

Kim goes back to standing with her husband, who wraps her in his arms. "You're welcome. I will always try my best to keep my people safe." I point to Madi. "She more than most, but it's time for us to go. We will meet you at your house at dawn. We have things to discuss."

I take a deep breath and then turn to face what I had done. I must walk past them to exit the clearing. Brand new shifters don't like to accept anyone but immediate family too close. In order to walk around, I have to go past the bodies. My whole body shudders.

These two witches happen to be the first people I have killed in this lifetime or even the last, but I am no stranger to death. Being hunted like we are, we have killed before, and I am sure there will be a need again in the future. That is just the way of life for shifters. It's a dangerous world out there.

Once at the bodies, I then step right over the top of them. As soon as we are out of sight of the Millers, I change shape again to the black shaggy Newfoundland. Tigers are not native to this area. Seeing one would cause problems and a lot of unwanted questions.

When we get to the car, Hunter opens the back door for me. I climb in and settle down on the rear seat. He closes my door and then gets in himself. We make our way back to my parents' house mostly in silence.

After everything we have been through tonight, I am exhausted. We will need at least a nap before the Millers return home at dawn. Then we will need to head straight back home. We have so much to do.

I stand up on the back seat as Hunter pulls into my parents' driveway. He opens the door for me, and we make our way inside. My parents are in bed, so the house is silent. I shift back to human as soon as we are in my room.

What seemed like three heartbeats later, Hunter woke me. I open my eyes to find light filtering in through the open curtains. It doesn't seem like we were here long at all. That doesn't matter, though. We shower and dress before making our way hand in hand down to the Millers.

As we walk, I dial my grandmother's number. "Good morning, Cady." She cheerfully answers on the second ring.

"It's definitely morning." I sigh.

Her tone changes. "What happened? Are you okay?" I hear something clatter on the other end of the line. "Do you need help? I cannot be there myself, but I can call in someone if needed."

I shake my head even though she can't see me. "Sorry, I'm just tired," I tell her. "Something did happen." We make our way up to the Miller's porch. They are not back yet, so we settle ourselves on their porch swing. "Do you remember my best friend, Madison?"

"Yes, she is the reason that you didn't want to come here in the first place." She says kindly. She is not judging me, just stating a fact.

"That's her. Well, I knew that she was going to change last night, and I had a funny feeling that something was going to happen. So, I followed them. Hunter and I did." I pause because I know that I should not have done that. A moonlight ceremony is normally a private event; unless invited, you stay away.

My grandmother doesn't say anything; she knows I know what I did was a no-no. "It turns out that it was a good thing I did. Three witches, sent by Felicia, were there. I killed two and let one go back to his master to send a message."

"Is anyone hurt?" she asks. "This is what I was showing you the other day. Those photos were taken in places known to be used for moonlight." She confirmed my earlier suspicions.

"No one is hurt. I have some glass in my side..."

"Do what? Why didn't you tell me?" Hunter interrupts me.

"It's fine. It is already working its way out of my body. It's just a sliver," I tell Hunter. "The Millers are all safe. We left after making sure there were no more surprises." I laugh. "After Madi changed, which she was seconds from finishing when we left, I doubt anyone would mess with that huge bear."

She chuckles. "When are you coming back? What would you like me to do?"

I look up at Hunter. "I am not sure anyone is going to like this, but Hunter and I think it's best if, until we catch Felicia, all moonlight ceremonies are required to have a few extra guards. Larger animals, older ones. This way, the new shifters have a little extra backup."

"You are correct. No one is going to like this at all. I can make some phone calls, but I promise that most will refuse."

I nod more to myself than to her. "Well, too bad. Tell them I, without telling them who I am, am ordering this for the time being. Felicia now knows the Black Dawn is coming for her. I will, too. I will not stop until she is no longer able to prey on our kind."

The Millers' car is coming up the road, so I need to speed this up. "If you will please start making the calls, we are about to have a conversation with the Millers, and I will be bringing Madi with us. We should be on the road within a couple of hours." I end the call and stand.

As soon as Madi is out of the car, she is running at me. She throws her arms around me. "Oh, Cady," she cries. I hug her back as tight as I can. I whisper assurances to her just to calm her down.

Kim and Dale join us on the porch. "Let's go inside," Dale says as he unlocks the door. Madi lets go of my body, but she keeps my hand, like she does not want to face whatever we are going to talk about alone. I will be with her; she has no worries. I will not leave her behind.

We step inside to find the remaining mess from the party. That seems like so long ago now, even though it was just a few hours. We all get settled in the living room. Hunter, Madi, and I are all on the couch, and the Millers are on the loveseat.

They wait, knowing that this is my show. "I want to take Madi with me back to the Farm," I drop the bomb.

Chaos unfolds, just like I expected. However, two hours later, Madi is passed out in the back seat of my car, and we are well on our way back to the Farm.

CHAPTER TWENTY-NINE

Hunter

Madison slept for most of the drive back to Texas and was still passed out when we got to the Farm. Some of the staff came to get our stuff from the car. Cadence and I are just standing here looking down at Madi.

"We can't leave her in the car," Cady tells me, stating the obvious.

"I will take her up." I leaned down to kiss her lips. "You go talk to your grandparents, and I will meet you in your...our room."

"Thank you, baby," she says and makes her way inside.

Leaning down and slipping one arm under Madison's head and one under her legs. It is awkward for a few moments because I have to almost crawl all the way into the back seat to reach her. Once I am out of the car, I adjust her where I am carrying her princess style. I kick the car door closed with my foot.

Madison is completely knocked out. She didn't wake wake up once—not getting her out of the car, or going up the stairs, or even getting her into her new bed.

Not sure if she would remember the conversation from before she fell asleep in the car, so I left her a note letting her know that if she needed anything, we would be next door, or Anna was only two doors down.

Once she is situated and knows how to find us when she wakes up all alone in a strange bed in a strange house, I make my way over to my old room in the visitor section of the house.

It doesn't take me long to pack all my belongings back up. I really only have a few things here. That will have to change once all of this mess with Felicia is settled. Once we figure out where we are staying for good, I will then bring all of my stuff from the storage that is normally stored between lifetimes to wherever we settle.

I make my way back across the house and walk in to find Cady has just returned. "Thanks again for getting Madi to her room. I stopped and checked on her."

I figured she would. She would not be able to sleep until she had seen that her best friend was settled. I just smile at her. She is so cute when she is being so predictable.

"Do you want to shower?" I asked, already knowing the answer. I start for the bathroom. She follows without another word. After that many hours stuck in a car, a shower was definitely in order, especially after the battle of sorts that she fought.

Within thirty minutes, we are clean and lying in bed side by side naked, just the way we like it. Cadence's back is snuggled up against my chest, and my arm is wrapped around her waist, holding her close. Nothing feels better in this world than the feel of my mate's skin against mine.

Cadence wiggles her behind as if she is trying to get comfortable, but I know my mate. This has nothing to do with her position and everything to do with what is now firmly pressing against her backside, growing firmer with every wiggle of her ass.

All of a sudden, she turns around to face me and throws one knee up over my hip. She kisses my lips, softly at first, and she lets her feelings in this moment pour from not only her lips but her mind as well, linking us completely. I can feel what she feels, and I suspect that she can as well.

She touches my face with just the tips of her fingers and lightly scrapes her nails through the stubble on my jaw. Slowly, she runs those nails down my neck, letting her lips follow in their wake.

When she gets to my chest, she pushes me back, and I allow her to push me onto my back. I want to see where she is going with this, even though I am still firmly in her mind.

My entire body shudders with need as she continues downward with nails and lips following my happy trail. I bunch her hair in my fist so I can watch her face as she kisses her way down to my groin.

Blood pounds through my cock at the first touch of her small hand. My heartbeat is centered completely in my cock. Every cell. My body feels alive, like a live wire has attached itself to me. There is a strange roaring in my ears. My body thrums with anticipation as she leans over me. I can feel her hot breath on my bare skin.

"Cadence..." Her name comes out as a plea when it was meant as a command. A powerful one. Only it came out hoarse, almost desperate, and not sounding like me at all. Not nearly as authoritative as I intended. It just shows how desperate I really am.

Her warm breath slides over me again, this time deliberate, so that my muscles tighten instantly. She lifts her eyes to meet mine again. There is a note of mischief in her small smile. There is a dark hunger and intense desire in her eyes. I absolutely love that look. It makes small droplets leak out of the crown of my cock.

This entices her. She licks up the length of my shaft, taking the drops of precum as she comes to the head, then stops to savor the taste of me as I lie here watching her.

In this moment, there is only us. The world falls away. There are no Farm or shifters in the next room. There is no duty and no war to win. Nothing beyond the four walls around us. Every problem can wait. It no longer matters. There is only Cadence and how her hot, wet mouth feels engulfing my cock in one go. All sane thought evaporates.

She slides her mouth down my length with her lips pressed tight. Her tongue strokes and dances as she takes me straight down her throat.

She moans softly, sending a vibration right through my shaft, straight to my balls. It is the sexiest thing I have ever seen. Her lashes drop as she focuses on her task.

"Eyes on me, love."

Her long lashes lift again as her hand slides up the twin columns of my thighs in a slow, burning slide. Then her fingers tentatively stroke over my straining balls. My breath that I hadn't realized I was holding left my lungs in a rush.

The entire time, I keep my gaze locked on her gorgeous eyes. She looks stunning with my cock down her throat, with the love she has for me shining clearly in her green eyes.

As she comes back up for much-needed air, I pull her all the way off my cock and throw her on the bed in my place. She lands on her back, and I place my hands on her knees and spread her wide apart for me.

I can see the evidence of what she has done to me all over her thighs and her soaking wet folds.

My cock is thick, aggressive, and I'm not sure I could get any harder without bursting. I rest the crown right at her scorching hot entrance. She won't stop moving her hips trying to impale herself, so I slide my hands to her hips to hold her in place.

"Hunter..." Cadence begs. My gaze is holding her captive as I thrust forward, driving right through her tight folds, which seems to narrow to accommodate my thick girth, even though she is slick and welcoming. Her walls clamped down around my cock, making it hard to push through her wet heat.

My mind is still firmly in hers, and I can feel the pressure of my thrust from both sides. She must be able to as well because her body answers by gripping me tighter.

Her nails rake up my arms and across my back as I pull back to thrust back into her again. This time, sliding a bit further inside of her. In and out of her tight channel like a madman. I can never get enough of my mate. The friction seems to increase as she starts to lift her hips to match my thrust for thrust.

Her nails dig into the skin of my back, scoring down as I ride her mercilessly. Harder and faster until I can feel the walls of her tighten down on me. "Thank fuck," I say as she explodes around me, milking my own release from my body. I ride it out as the thick jets coat her insides, filling her with my seed.

For a while, there are just the sounds of our combined breathing filling the room. Once I am able, I pull out of her slowly and collapse on the bed beside her. I pull her to me, and we are both out within seconds.

Chapter Thirty

Cadence

"Dᴏ ʏᴏᴜ ɢᴇᴛ ɪᴛ?" *I hear the question asked from my own mouth, but the voice is not mine. It does not belong to me. I can tell that I am not myself. I am in a female's body. The voice that came out of my mouth belongs to a female, a female that should be long dead by now, and if I have my way, she will be very soon.*

Somehow, I am in the body, living in this moment as my biggest enemy. I have somehow connected to Felicia. The very witch that has tried everything in her power to exterminate my species, all the while stealing from us.

Many moons ago, when the witch was young, long before she turned evil, she was only just another person. She fell in love with the boy next door. Cecil was everything to her; only a year apart in age, they were to be wed as soon as she turned eighteen. Only, instead of getting married to her beloved, he revealed he was a shifter and had found his mate.

Cecil and Edith ran off together, leaving Felicia a broken shell of herself. That day, she vowed to destroy not only Cecil and the bitch that stole the love of her life from her, but she would exterminate every last shifter in the world.

The day she used the spell to kill those two, her soul turned black and died. It changed something deep inside of her very core. She stopped aging as soon as she took their lives. However, it didn't last long. When she started aging again, she started killing more and more shifters.

She soon found out that no matter what she did, she could not combine the longevity of more shifters. For every shifter killed with the spell, she would gain about a fortnight. Every fourteen days, she would need to repeat the spell and kill another shifter.

"Yes, ma'am." The male's voice pulls me from my thoughts and brings me back to the here and now.

I am standing in a large open room in what appears to be a small hut. It looks more like a shack; however, two doorways lead off from this room. The walls are lined with shelves, and several cross-body bags that look full of something are sitting in one corner.

A young woman is standing next to me who cannot be over five and a half feet tall. She is slender with blonde hair cut in a pixie style. A male has just entered the room, with a small canvas bag in his hands.

The male who had spoken is a tall, lean man with black shaggy hair. He hands me—Felicia—a brown cloth bag.

She takes the bag and opens it to reveal green leaves. The bag is full, but she only removes two leaves with a large smile on her face. I can feel the smile lighting up her entire face. "This will make so many batches, giving us the advantage of weakening them before the big one. Once I get the last items I need." She hands the bag off to the female beside her.

Right in front of Felicia is a huge cast-iron cauldron. She takes the few steps she needs to reach the pot of boiling liquid. The liquid inside is a light blue color, and I can see the bubbles creating foam on top.

She tosses the newest leaves into the pot and laughs with glee. "They will never know what hit them." She turns to face the other two in the room. Hannah and Garen are their names. I can see from Felicia's mind that they are her most trusted witches. The only two she would share with them in the end.

She looks back behind her at the pot. "Do you have the antidote to the acid fog ready?"

It is Hannah who answers her. "Yes, it is ready for us when we need it. When we coat our clothes and skin, it will keep us from being affected."

She faces Garan. "What about the other things I asked for?"

He looks down at the phone in his hands. He scrolls for a moment. "She said they have acquired the items and are on their way back. They should be back two days from now."

A beeping sound pulls me from the small hut, placing me back in my own body. Hunter is still beside me. He reaches over to shut off the alarm as I sit up.

I try to remember all the details of what I just witnessed. This is very important. "We have a new problem," I tell Hunter. "I am not sure what to do about it."

He stands and comes to my side of the bed. "What happened?" Just like that, he is there, never even doubting that I know what I'm talking about.

I tell him about what I had just seen and heard while I was in Felicia's body. "Acid fog," I repeat to myself. "We have nothing that will work against that."

Hunter is quiet for a while, but then shrugs. "You are correct. So, we just move on and keep going." He leans down and kisses my forehead. "Let's go eat. Then I would like to see if we can call on that fire again."

After we eat, we make our way back out to where we have designated our private training area. Since we are the only ones to ever come here, it is ours—at least until my secret is out.

As I disrobe, Hunter does not take his eyes off me. "Shift into your panther, please."

I do as I am asked and look down to see my normal paws. Just the black fur with the dark grey semicircles. I look back at my mate, who is still standing in human form.

"A lot of times, shifters' instincts are based on feelings," he reminds me. "Now I want you to try to remember what you were feeling when you turned into the Hellcat."

Honestly, I was scared shitless. So scared that I cannot really describe what I was feeling. I knew they had come for my bestie, and if I didn't do something, I would lose not only her but two people who were like another set of parents to me. They have been in my life more than even my own grandparents.

I blink up at Hunter. "Close your eyes," he tells me. I do as he says and just listen to the sound of his voice. "I want you to clear your mind completely."

I lay my body on the ground, keeping my eyes closed. I start counting my breaths, trying to completely relax. Once I had found my Zen, I waited.

"Now think back to Madi's birthday." He pauses. "We followed in your car and then went on foot. We watched and saw three extra people there."

I try to do as he says and think. We are doing something we shouldn't be doing, but we are there anyway. I picture the witches coming out of the trees, potions ready.

"They are coming for the Millers. They are coming for Madi, your best friend, your sister." He stops again as I follow along. "They are going to kill her," he raises his voice in false alarm. "That's it!"

I opened my eyes to see smoke coming up from my paws, but no flame. I looked up at Hunter. "*What happened?*"

"You flickered for a moment, but it went right back out. Try again."

So, I did. Over and over until I couldn't do it anymore. I shift back to human form. "I need fuel."

We head back to the house to find that we completely missed lunch. We end up with cold cut sandwiches and water bottles. We make our way back outside to find Anna and Madi coming back from the training grounds.

"Where have y'all been?" Anna asks. "More secret training?"

I laugh. "Yep. Unfortunately, I have to go back too. Trying to figure this out, but I would love to meet up with everyone for supper." I look up at Hunter. "Does that sound good to you?"

He nods. "That sounds great. I am hoping we can figure this fire thing out soon." He takes my plate and water. "I'll take these to the table."

I turned back to the girls. "Still can't figure out how you turned into a flaming cat?" Madi asks. She only knows because I had to explain after everything went down. She was too far into her first shift to know anything other than the fact that there were extra voices that she did not recognize.

I sigh. "No! I can't figure it out." I pause. "I know." I smile, feeling like a light bulb has gone off above my head, like in the cartoons I used to watch as a kid. "Maybe you two can help. You are the only ones who know about me." I whisper the last part.

They exchange a look and then shrug. "What are you thinking?" Anna asks.

Right then, Travis walks out the door behind me before I could answer. "Hey, girls." He looks at me. "I see you are back. You missed lunch. What are you being so secretive about? We all know you shift into a dog, but I have only seen you shift once."

I look at the girls, then back to Travis. I blink. I can't tell him anything. Madi saves me like always. "Nothing secret. She just wants alone time with her mate." She giggles.

"Who wouldn't want alone time with that sexy beast?" Anna adds fanning herself dramatically.

I blush on cue, making myself appear shy and embarrassed.

Travis holds his hands up in surrender. "I do not want to know more." He laughs. "See you later." He walks away, leaving us alone again.

"Oh my goddess. That was close. Thanks, guys," Hunter calls my name. "I'd better go eat. Give us twenty minutes and meet us back here. Please be prepared to shift." I jog off to get my cold lunch down before we have to go back.

I fill Hunter in on the plan as we eat our food. Twenty minutes later, all four of us are loaded up in the ATV and headed to the back of the property.

Once we are situated in our training spot, I had Anna shift and chase Madi in human form, not even thinking about their size difference.

When that didn't work, they switched roles. It works a lot better when the bear is chasing the tiny dog. I shifted and once again tried to find my calm.

After several failed attempts, we all shift back to our human forms and just lean against the massive fence. "I don't get it," I tell them with a sigh. I am starting to get mad at myself.

Madi's sidearm hugs me from the left side. Anna sees what she is doing and does the same on the right. Both of my best friends are offering me some support.

"How am I going to defeat Felicia when I can't even..." I trail off as the world goes dark. The girls and Hunter are completely gone. I am no longer seeing the backside of the Farm's property.

No... Now I am back in what appears to be the little hut where Felicia has camped out. This time I am in a sitting room. This room is just as big as the last, but there are couches. Old, crusty couches that look like they have been abandoned for the wild animals.

The main couch looks like those old floral couches that everyone hated, but they would fold out into a bed, so they ended up being in many homes. The beds were hard and thin. You could feel every bar of the fold-out frame. The white between the flowers was now a dull grey.

There is a loveseat that sits near the couch, but far enough away to be able to open the main couch into a bed. It was in worse shape. There were holes in the cushions and back where it appeared an animal had scratched at it so much that most of the stuffing was all gone.

On the loveseat, Hannah and Garan sat, looking relaxed, as if they have spent a lot of time here. There didn't appear to be anyone else in the room—just the three of them. There was yet another pot or cauldron hanging over the fireplace. This one was a lot smaller than the last one. It was boiling, as was the last.

"It's almost ready," Hannah told Felicia while looking at the pot, bringing my attention back to the occupants in the room.

Felicia rubbed her hands together excitedly. "Finally, I will be done with this. My immortality is within reach."

The other smiled back at her. I can tell that Felicia has promised to share the new immortality spell with the two of them. "We just need to figure out who the Black Dawn is," Garan stated.

Hannah looked down at her cell phone again. "Our source..." She pauses to laugh. "...says that he believes the Black Dawn is in the Houston area, most likely being hidden at the place they call The Farm."

Felicia and Garen nod. "Good. Once the last spell is complete, we will take the fight to them." She looks at Garan. "Tell me what the experiments have yielded."

Garen pulls out a folder that was sitting beside him and opens it. "This new potion is even better than the last." He pulls one paper out of the folder. "Once activated, it will remove the ability to shift just like the last one, but this one will remain in their system for three days."

"Fantastic, that will level the playing field. When will we have enough to take into battle?" Felicia responds.

I didn't catch the answer because I felt something pushing on me. Instantly, I threw my hands up to protect myself from whatever was attacking me. As I opened my eyes, I saw that I was once again back in my own body. Madi and Anna were throwing themselves sideways as a huge ball of fire soared past them straight for the ATV.

The fireball that I had somehow conjured and thrown at my besties when they startled me is barreling toward the ATV with no way to stop it. As it hits its unintended targets, the entire thing is instantly engulfed in flames.

All of us turned to run, but before we could get more than thirty steps away, the ATV exploded, sending us flying through the air to land in a heap.

I look around to see that my mate and my friends are all in one piece. Anna has a small cut on her forehead that is trickling down her face at a steady rate, but that seems to be the only injury. All four of us are covered in a fine black soot.

Before we can do much more than pick ourselves up off the ground, our little private oasis is invaded by shifters. There are about fifty of them, the beta male in the lead. "What the hell happened here?" He wasn't even looking at the ATV. He was looking at the huge hole in the wall behind us.

Chapter Thirty-One

Cadence

Jameson leads the four of us into the house. He does just as I asked him to do. He treated us just like he would any other group of new shifters. He led us all prisoner-style through the house, stopping only long enough to allow us to grab some food that the staff was already starting to put away.

He then leads us straight to the conference room, where we would have plenty of privacy for the conversation ahead. "Have a seat." He tells us. "I will go get Rose, Robert, and Emily while you eat." He hands us a package of wet wipes on his way out the door.

We all use the wipes to clean our hands and as much of our faces as we can. We didn't really want to eat without a shower, but this meeting was too important to postpone.

Just as we are finishing up, the conference room door opens again. To be fair, we all ate quickly. It had only been about ten minutes since Jameson left us in here.

My grandparents and the betas come in and sit at the table. They look us all over. They can see all the soot that still covers our bodies. The wipes wouldn't be able to remove all of it. I can see that the others have a black ring around their faces. They could see everything, even the now-healing cut on Anna's head and our disheveled overall appearance.

My grandmother returned her gaze to me. "Would you care to explain?"

I sheepishly smile. "I guess I have a new power."

"Other than the flaming cat you told us about?" My grandfather inquires.

I nod, then pause and tilt my head, thinking. "Well, maybe two," I add. The others are sitting quietly, letting me do all the talking. Since I am to be their leader, I guess I should get used to this.

"Two new powers?" Jameson asked. "I assume one is the reason we have a new hole in the west fence."

My grandparents' gaze snaps to him. Apparently, he didn't inform them of what had happened. "Cadence…" He looks at me. "… you better tell them what happened."

Their eyes come back to settle on mine. "So, you know that during Madi's moonlight, we interrupted an attack, sent for the Millers, and you know that I turned into the fiery beast. A hellcat." I pause, and they nod. "What you do not know is I have no clue how to bring it back."

"That is not uncommon with new shifters," Emily adds. "You would think it would be the same with these new powers."

I smile in thanks to her. "Also, what you don't know is that I have connected to Felicia twice now. Mentally, that is. But I will get to that in a minute."

Every face at the table, except Hunter's, showed different degrees of shock. I don't give them time to cut in, though. "We were out there trying to figure out a way to bring the hellcat back. We…" I motion to Hunter. "Have been trying all day with no luck."

I growl under my breath as I am still upset with myself for not being able to figure this out.

"Well, when we shifted back to human, we were resting against the wall. We were exhausted from all the shifting. I am thinking that's one of the reasons I connected back to Felicia. Again, I will tell you about both times in a second. I talked to them about this while we were eating." I look at the girls, then back to my grandparents.

"They said that my eyes glazed over, and I just froze. They tried talking to me, but I wouldn't respond. They got worried. Because I was not answering, they tried to shake me." I go on. "Well, this startled me out of the connection, making me think I was being attacked. I threw my hands up to protect myself, and a giant ball of fire flew from my hands. It was headed right for the girls. They managed to move out of the way in time, but it instead went straight for the ATV, making it explode."

"I see." My grandfather says, at the same time as my grandmother says. "What about the visions or whatever happened with Felicia?"

Jameson nods. "I agree with Rose. This is what we need to know. The fence or the ATV is not important at this time." Everyone agrees.

I take a deep breath. This right here is the reason we needed this meeting. "First, I need to know what the emergency protocols are."

My grandparents and the betas exchange a worried look. "That doesn't sound good." Emily says. I shake my head, but wait for my grandparents to answer.

"That depends on how big the emergency is," she informs me.

"The biggest."

"Well, we can call an emergency summit meeting. Almost like the one you joined in on before."

"How much time do we have?" I love my grandfather's no-bullshit attitude. He is straight to the point.

I think about that for a moment. "I am not completely sure. Maybe twelve hours if—and I specify if—we are lucky."

"Shit!" That is the only answer I get. My grandmother doesn't ask if I am sure or question me at all. She picks up the phone beside her on the table and presses a button. "Code Black!" she says into the receiver and then hangs up.

Not thirty seconds later, a woman in her forties rushes in with a black binder in her hands. She gives the binder to my grandmother, and then she is gone again.

My grandmother opens the binder and takes out the papers, handing one to my grandfather, one to each of the betas, and one to me. The girls leave to start their showers as I look down at the paper now in my hands.

It is instructions on what procedures should be used in a case of a Code Black. It also has the contact information for the Southern leader, Carlos.

Hunter reads over my shoulder. "I can call Franklin." My grandfather nods and hands him a piece of paper from the binder.

I pull my cell phone from the pocket of my robe. Thankfully, it is intact after the explosion. I enter the number from the information sheet in front of me.

The phone is answered on the fourth ring. Then a female voice comes on the line. "Hello, this is Carlos's phone. May I help you?"

That throws me for a moment. I was expecting the Southern leader himself to answer the phone. "Hello, my name is Cadence, and I need to speak with Carlos immediately."

"He is in a meeting right now. Can I take a message?" Her voice is already getting on my nerves. She is too chipper, but it is a fake chipper, if that is possible. The type of voice someone uses when they answer the phone to a stranger.

"You need to bring him the phone, right this second. This is more important than any meeting he could be attending."

"I am sorry, I can..." She starts at the same time as Hunter whispers to me. "Tell her the code."

"I have a Code Black." I cut her off.

She starts to stutter. "Yes, ma'am." I hear a light knock on wood, then Carlos's voice. "I thought I told you I did not want to be disturbed."

"I am sorry, Sir, but I have a Cadence on the phone with a Code Black. The ID says central region."

There is some rustling. Then I hear a voice on the line. "Did I hear her correctly?" Carlos adds to the phone.

"Yes. We have a Code Black in Texas at the Farm."

"How long?"

"Less than twelve hours," I informed him. "I am not altogether certain, but it will not be after that."

"I am on my way," he says, then hangs up the phone. Short, sweet, to the point.

I look up only to find Jameson still on the phone. "I cannot reach the Eastern leader. He is not answering any of his contact numbers," he tells us.

I didn't really expect him to anyway. "I will tell you about the visions or whatever happened while I was connected to Felicia," I tell them about both. "We can expect all older potions and spells, as well as the new acid fog and the newest, to stop us from shifting. Felicia and her two besties will be coming for me. They want me alive. I can use this to my advantage."

We finish up, then go our separate ways. We will all do what we needed for the battle ahead. After the day, a shower and a nap are on that list.

— ⋇ —

"Felicia, I have Great news." A man comes running up to a group of people. A large group. The man who is just coming up looks vaguely familiar, but I cannot figure out where.

The group of people is standing outside the little hut that I have seen both times. It's not really a hut. I can tell from this angle. It is a small house. It is just run down a lot. With white chipping paint and what was once bright blue trim.

The house itself is surrounded by trees. The property must be located inside a grove. I can see nothing else of the surrounding area other than a dirt driveway that leads out of the area.

Felicia turns to face the newcomer but doesn't say anything. She just waits expectantly.

"I know you plan to come in from the north side of the Farm, but there happens to be a brand-new hole in the fence on the west side."

Felicia just stands there thinking. Then she turns to Garen. "If we use the hole that is already there, our entrance would be silent. Is this possible?"

Garan turns to look at a map that is laid out on a small fold-up table behind him. It looks like a little foldable card table. He points at it. "Yes, that could work." He points to something else on the map and runs his finger along the line. "We can use this route to get there. Then come up in the empty field behind the Farm."

"Great! Since we'll be going in silently, we can catch more of them still sleeping." Felicia turns to look at the other man, who is way too old to be on the battlefield. "How long until we are ready?"

He appears to be in his sixties. He straightens his shoulders. "We should be good to go within the hour." He looks down at the map in front of Garen. "That should put us at the Farm about five." He holds his hand out flat, then rocks it back and forth. "Give or take."

This time, I know I am in the connection, and I know I need to get out right this very second. I push myself out of the connection to find myself back in my bed with Hunter still sleeping soundly.

I glance at the bedside table, at the digital clock. It reads two o'clock in the morning. "Shit. Shit. Shit! Hunter, wake up, we have to go." I sit up on the side of the bed. "Heads up, try to block yourself, or I will blast your head."

I wait until he nods. Then send the message to all shifters telepathically. *"Attention, everyone."* I paused to give people a second to wake up. We don't have much more time than that. *I need every shifter within hearing distance to meet me in the courtyard immediately. I do mean every single shifter. If you can hear me, you have ten minutes."*

"What's happening?" Hunter asked. But he is already dressing.

I shake my head at him. "Your robe, please." My voice wavers slightly, but he doesn't comment. This entire thing is on my shoulders to lead. No, I won't be fighting alone, but my anxiety is through the roof right now. "Can we do this? Can we win?" My hands shake and I press them against the side of my robe.

Hunter comes up and wraps his arms around me. "You, my love, are the Black Dawn. You can do anything you put your mind to. I will be right there with you. I believe in you." He presses his lips to mine pouring all his confidence into me with that one all to short kiss.

"We are out of time. They are coming now," I whisper. "We have no choice but to go and face them, no matter the outcome."

We head straight out to the courtyard, pushing our way through bodies. We find several people are already there, including my grandparents. I make a beeline straight to them. More and more people are crowding around us as we make our way across this space.

"What's going on?" my grandmother asks, but by the look on her face, she already knows.

I nod at her look and then turn to look around us. The courtyard is filling fast and starting to spill out into the yard beyond. "Who all has made it?" I ask; I need to know that all will be able to fight.

"Jameson, status report!" My grandfather barks. Gone is the sweet, loving grandfather I have always known, in his place as the leader of the Central Region.

The beta steps forward. "The Western leader arrived about an hour ago. She should be here..." He trails off to search the area." There she is." I turned to see Sarah. She is headed right for us. Her betas are bringing up the rear.

She stops in front of us. "Who has the audacity to call us in that manner? I understand this is a Code Black, but no one orders me to do anything," she says with a sneer.

Wow, this version of Sarah is the complete opposite of the woman I met at the Summit meeting. It makes me wonder which is the real Sarah McClain.

I step right up into her personal space. "*I have the audacity,*" I tell her telepathically, sending it only to her.

Her mouth drops, and she steps back. "You..." She stutters on a whisper. "You..." She repeats louder. She bends slightly at the waist and then straightens. The action is not missed by her beta pair.

By this time, the ten minutes that I have given the shifters are up. I turned to survey the crowd. I have never seen so many shifters in one place. There are people of all shapes and sizes.

Everyone is talking at once. There is no way I will be heard over the noise. I look around again. I see Elena making her way over to us as well. As she passes, so many are asking her questions.

I decide that I need to get higher so I can get everyone's attention. With Hunter's help, I climb up on the picnic table behind us. Weirdly enough, it is our normal table.

Once I am up where everyone can see me, the noise level actually increases with everyone shouting questions. "*Everyone, quiet.*" I pushed directly into their minds. As everyone goes quiet other than a baby crying somewhere in the crowd, I start again. "Hello, everyone," I say out loud now that they can hear me. "I am sure a lot of you are wondering what you are doing here and who I am." I look around at everyone. "Let me introduce myself." Switching back to telepathy. "*I am Cadence Robinson, the Black Dawn.*"

The murmurs go up again. I give them a moment while I locate Emily. "Can you escort all the children under the age of fifteen and any other vulnerable people to the safe room in Granny's office? Please come back prepared to shift. We need every able-bodied person to fight."

I turn back to the crowd. "Emily here is going to take all the children, any pregnant or injured, or any not able to fight to a safe room that was built right here at the Farm for this reason." They do not have to know that the safe room was actually built for me.

Once they cleared out, I started again. Now, as for why we are here, Felicia and so many of her people are on their way here right this second. She is planning to kill every man, woman, and child. Of any shifter she finds."

It starts to get loud again. I have to remind them once again to stay quiet, at least low enough that everyone can hear. "They are not only bringing numbers, but at least two new potions. Potion one will hurt physically. The other one will remove your ability to shift." There is no need to tell them about the third. I am the only one in danger of that one. This time, I give them a moment to have their outrage.

"We do not have long. They are planning to come through the hole I accidentally put in the west wall. Taking us out by surprise when we are all in bed sleeping." I pause. "I don't like that plan. So, we will bring the fight to them. In the clearing at the back of the property."

I then turned to my grandparents. "I want all fifteen- to seventeen-year-olds on the hole, with a small team with them. Can you take care of that?"

Once they take off to do as I ask, I turn back to the crowd. "I want us to fight in teams when we can. That way, you always have someone watching your back. This is going to be a long, hard battle, but it is one we have to win. There is no other choice. We have dealt with this enemy long enough. It is time to end this madness once and for all."

They cheer. Then I turn to Elena and Sarah. "Will you two make sure everyone has a battle buddy, even if it is an odd-numbered group. No one fights alone."

"Please get prepared. Then meet us at the west wall. As soon as you are ready. Remember, we need everyone, no matter what your animal."

CHAPTER THIRTY-TWO

Cadence

As I walk through the crowd surrounding the hole in the West side of the wall. I shrug off all lingering doubts. Now is the time for full confidence. I cannot... No, I will not allow myself to falter. There is no room for hesitation or uncertainty.

Either I can't defeat her, or I will allow her to kill all those around me and myself for her immortality. I know that Felicia is extremely dangerous. Even more so with her newest potions. I will not underestimate her again. Too many times, in the past lifetimes, I have done just that. Not this time.

I will have to allow all the other shifters to focus on her followers because my sole purpose is to focus on Felicia. It is my responsibility as the Black Dawn to take out the biggest threat to our people.

I let my breath out slowly. I have to believe in myself, believe in what the Goddess has gifted me. There is absolutely no time for second-guessing myself.

I will not let my people down. I repeat this as I pass through the crowd of shifters gathered, ready to go to war with me. Trusting in me to do my job. They watch me with confidence but also fear. There is no going back. You know, either we win, or we die.

As I make my way to what will be the front lines, I turn to look over everyone gathered.

The area leaders are standing in front. As is their rightful place. As area leaders, it is also their job to protect their people. Any area leader not willing to stand up for their people and their species shouldn't be a leader of any kind.

Behind the area leaders, groups are standing together everywhere. Hunter and Travis, Anna and Madi, Adam and Mack, Jameson and Emily, Koni and Kai, from the Southern region. Eric and Jonathan from the Western. Those are just in the front lines, right behind the area leaders. There are so many more groups standing behind them.

Just as I'm about to address the crowd once again, a line of vans comes around the corner of the fence. It stops right before the crowd. We all take up defensive positions, not knowing who the vans belong to. Not even knowing if Felicia changed her plans without me knowing it.

The first van stops. The closest to us. Out steps not only the Southern leader, Carlos, but also Franklin from the north. There are about ten vans in total. Where so many people are getting out and joining the groups. A wave of relief washes over me. Just these few extra people may push the battle a little more into our favor.

"Are we too late to join the party?" Carlos says with his southern accent.

"Just in time, guys. Join us up here," my grandfather tells him.

"All the others pair up. Everyone fights this battle with a buddy." Hunter adds.

They do as asked. I looked down at my phone to check the time. Then turn back to the shifters relying on me. I hear my Grandparents filling in the Northern and Southern leaders.

"By now, everyone here knows who I am." I send to all the surrounding shifters telepathically. This close to time, I don't want to raise my voice and possibly be overheard by anyone else.

"I know no one wants to go into battle today, but Felicia has taken that choice away from us. Today will not be easy. We may lose a few or even be affected by the acid fog potions they have, but as a group, we will win today. We will live to tell our stories and make any other future enemies think twice about messing with us. We will be the victors. So, put your game faces on, folks. It's time to play."

Silent cheers went up around the group, then almost everyone shifted at once, leaving only the area leaders and me in human form. Once they are fully animals, I look out over them. *"Positions, everyone."* Then I look to the area leaders. *"Y'all ready?"* I get the affirmative I need, or close enough, then turn to make my way across the field. When we reach the center, we stop facing the trees and wait.

From where we are and where I suspect Felicia and her minions will come out, according to the map Garan was using, we will be right in front of them. Felicia will only see the area leaders and me. Everyone else has scattered. In the hopes of giving us an advantage. Any advantage we can get.

"Cady, can you hear me?" I hear Mack's voice hesitate in my head.

"Yes. Mack, go ahead. What do you see?"

"Trouble. I see trouble. I see Felicia's group, and there are so many people with her." She starts to freak out a little in my head.

"Focus, Mackenzie." Adam's voice comes next. *"They are headed right for you."* He adds to me.

"How long? And how many?" I asked him.

"ETA is about three minutes before you see the first of them. As for how many... Hundreds. We are easily outnumbered." I can hear his nerves and his voice. He is also freaking out a little.

"We knew this could happen. Good job, guys. Now, each of you go to help our friends."

I turned to look at the area leaders. "Three minutes," I whisper. *"Hunter... Kai... Sophia, start picking as many off as you can from the back. Stealthy for now."*

Right on time with Adam's estimate, Felicia, Garan, and Hannah stepped out of the tree line in front of us. Luckily, there was only a small patch that was wide enough for three to be coming out at once, bottlenecking them in a sense.

Felicia keeps coming but does not use any of her potions yet. I can hear her speaking to the witches around her. Apparently, she wants to talk. Good. It will give the others time to start taking their numbers down from behind.

She stopped about fifty feet or so in front of me. Close enough to talk, but not close enough for a direct hit with any of the potion bottles she is carrying in her messenger bag. That is bulging. She came prepared.

"Well, it looks like you knew we were coming," she tells us as she looks over our small group, while hers keeps growing. I can see why Mack was freaking out. According to what I can already see, we are already outnumbered at least three to one.

Felicia's gaze stops at me. "Let me guess. The infamous Black Dawn?" she asked, but didn't wait for an answer. "You have to be her, but you are a puny thing for the so-called great one." I guess she thinks her teasing will get under my skin.

I just shrugged. She can think what she wants. "Yep. I am her," I state simply, using a bored tone. Anything to delay her from attacking is giving my shifters even another minute to get into their places.

"You don't think your measly seven shifters can defeat me. Do you? Not when I have so many..." She raises her arms to point out her massive army. "... friends that I have brought with me?" She is still using that condescending tone.

Just then, I hear several voices in my head at once. Since they are in animal form, they can still talk to me. "*Ready!*" I hear so many voices say at the same time that I smile.

"No," I answer Felicia, who starts to smile. "We don't have to defeat your army. We just have to defeat you." The smile drops from her face.

"You don't honestly think they will just allow you to waltz up here to me, do you?"

I shrug. "They will be too busy to worry about you," I tell Felicia, then telepathically to the shifters surrounding us. "*Now!*" I hear the area leaders behind me start to shift, then over a hundred animals step out of the trees, slowly stalking closer to the group of witches.

All hell breaks loose with a single curse and a premature discharge of an acid fog potion. I know it is acid fog because I can see the fog rolling in a four-foot path from the witch to the group of shifters in front of her, making all the shifters attack at once.

Felicia watches for a moment while the shifters collide with her witches. Then she says something I can't hear while turning back toward me. But the fireball I just threw in her direction is coming right for her. She avoids it by pulling a woman from beside her. She uses her like a shield in front of her body. The woman shrieks as she is engulfed in flames. Felicia watches as the flames take her life right in front of us.

While she is distracted, I shift, and surprise, surprise, I shift straight into the Hellcat form. That action alone has several sets of eyes, human and animal, shifting toward me.

One set of animal eyes is a wolf, which is hit with a glass vial while its attention is diverted. This one is not acid fog. No, because as soon as the glass breaks against his body and the yellow liquid inside touches his skin, he starts shifting back to human form.

The witch, thinking she just got an easy mark, moves in for the kill, only to be stopped by the wolf's partner. The very naked man picks up the dagger that the now-dead witch was holding, then turns back toward the fight.

I turned my attention back to Felicia. She is still staring at my flaming beast but snaps out of it fast. "*Keep Hannah and Garen off of me.*" I sent it to anyone able to help. As I stalk closer, I can see an eagle coming straight for Hannah's head.

The eagle's claws attached themselves to her hair, then lifted her completely off the ground as a tiger sneaks up behind her and closes its massive jaws around Hannah's head.

I can distinctly remember how that feels as well. To crush someone's head in your beast's mouth.

I can't focus on everyone else's battle when I have my own to fight. Felicia and Garen both throw a potion bottle at me at the same time, as if it were planned. Garry's bottle hits the ground in front of me, releasing the acid fog. It rolls and waves as if it's water across the ground towards me.

I sidestepped the bottle that Felicia threw, making the bottle soar past me. I hear the glass land and break on someone else behind me, but I cannot stop to see which area leader was just hit because the rolling smoke now rolls over my legs, hitting the fire coming from my paws.

I hear a hiss as the toxic smoke is devoured by the fire, leaving only a tingling feeling in my limbs. Garen is now engaged in battle with a black bear, leaving me to face Felicia alone.

Felicia just stumbles back, her eyes wide with shock and fear. She shrieks. She honestly came into this battle thinking she would sneak up on us to get an easy win. But whatever. The force that allowed me to connect physically and psychologically took away that dream.

Now there was nothing left but a flaming beast straight from Hell, staring her in the face, showing her exactly how hard her death was going to be.

With a flick of my tail that I once hated so much, I stepped forward toward her on sure feet, picking up speed. When I am within a dozen feet of her, I pounce.

She moves at the last minute, making me miss my mark. However, I was still able to graze her with my razor-sharp claws, swiping across her side before turning at the last moment to land on my feet.

While she is on the ground shrieking in pain, I catch movement out of the corner of my eye. I turned to see that a male had not only a potion bottle but a very small dog in his hands. I see that he tries to crush the dog, making the potion bottle shatter against her head. As the dog starts to shift, he throws the dog right at the bear, headed for him.

I lift my paw as if I could stop the witch from killing my friend. From this far away, only the fire that is attached to my paw splits in half, sending part of the flame straight for the witch. At the last second, it splits again, and I do not see where the other half went.

As he is encased in flames, I feel something stabs into my left flank. Turning, I see that Felicia has not only recovered but found a dagger somewhere and thrown it at my side.

The dagger has to have been spelled because as soon as it sinks into my back leg, it seems as if the last of my strength is leaking out right along with the blood. The flames that I was shrouded in flicker and goes out right before my eyes. I am still in animals form but just barely. The leg that she hit is like dead weight, completely useless.

I turned back to Felicia as I heard her rummaging through her messenger bag, which she still held on to while chanting softly. It seems she is going to attempt to steal my life and longevity right here on the battlefield. I guess she's decided she wouldn't be able to kidnap me.

The brief glance around told me that the battle was going in our favor for the moment. So, she no longer has a choice but to do it here.

I can't let that happen. If she does what she is trying to do, she will kill all that's left. Army or no army. It is my job to stop this and I am so close to failing. I have to give it one last try.

While she is still distracted, thinking I am down for the count, I gather the last of my strength without moving much. I don't want to draw her attention too soon. When I think I am able to, I jump one last time, aiming right for her head.

She looks up with wide eyes as I land right on top of her, locking my teeth around what I can reach of her face as my claws contact the soft flesh of her belly. I slipped in a scooping motion with my paws as I clamped my teeth. Down into her face.

She starts to scream, but it is cut off soon after as my canine teeth pierce her brain. If I thought the sound of just a head crushing was bad, that was nothing compared to this. Not only was there the crunch of bones, but the squishiness of the brain leaking into my mouth was disgusting.

The good thing was that no amount of longevity will allow anyone to live through that or the sliced intestines that are now lying on the ground in front of her.

I drop her body and look around once again. There are so many bodies on the ground that it is difficult to tell friend from foe.

I look around to try to find Hunter. I can't live without my mate. He has to be alive. I spot him battling a female witch with a large breed dog. This must be Travis. Before I can look away, I see Adam swoop down and claw the witch as Hunter slices the witch's throat.

I let out a sigh of relief, then turned my attention back to the battlefield as a whole. There are now large groups of shifters fighting witches tag team style, taking out the last of the two groups left.

The last remaining group sees they are the last man standing and turns around to flee, only to have a group that includes Madi and Mack attempting to stop them.

"*Let them go,*" I tell them. "*It's over.*"

Then I promptly pass out.

I wake sometime later with the sun shining in my eyes. I am back in my human form, covered in my own robe. The dagger is no longer in my leg, and I can feel my body trying to heal itself. I sit up and look around.

There are nowhere near as many people around me. I can see so many bodies, though.

Some are still scattered around the field, some are piled up, and there are even some leaning against the fence behind me. I can see about a dozen or so standing or moving around the field. Hunter and my grandparents are standing on the other side of the field talking.

I stand on shaky legs and make my way over to them, limping the entire way. "What's going on?" I asked as I walked up beside them.

They all turn to look at me. "What are you doing up on that leg, young lady?" My granny reprimands.

I wave that away. "I can heal later. Now I need a status report."

My grandfather sighs, knowing I will not move until I get what I want. "Most of the injured have been moved into the Infirmary." He points to a few people. I see someone leaning up against the fence. "That's all that's left."

"Dead?" I ask, knowing I've seen a few bodies that I know no one could survive the injuries.

They hang their heads in silence for a moment, then Hunter drops the bomb. "Fifty-seven." Shit, that is a lot of losses. We knew there were going to be losses, but that's still a big hit. "Northern had twenty-two lost shifters. The Southern region had twelve, the West had thirteen, including Sarah. The Central lost ten," he adds. "East had none, since they didn't show up."

That made me think about what I saw while I was battling Felicia. "Anna?" I need the answer, but I really didn't want to know if my friend didn't make it.

My granny steps up and wraps her arms over my shoulder. "She was hit with the anti-shift potion, so she can't shift, but unfortunately, one of your fireballs did hit her square in the chest."

"No!" I cry. "Please tell me I didn't kill my friend." Tears stream down my face as sudden grief overwhelms me. My knees slam into the ground jarring the wound on my leg. Oh God, what have I done?

"What are you crying about, you big baby? I know you saved the day and all, but that doesn't give you a free pass." Anna's voice comes from behind me.

I jump up, not caring about that. I reopen my wound on my leg and wrap her up in my arms, squeezing her tightly, too tightly if the tapping on my shoulder meant what I think it did. I pull back and look at her. She doesn't have a single burn on her. "I thought I killed you!" I exclaim. I wrap her in my arms again.

She pulls out of my arms, likely because I am hurting her again. "No, but my body ate that shit like it was breakfast. She rubs her belly. "Speaking of... Who's hungry?"

CHAPTER THIRTY-THREE

Cadence

AFTER EVERYONE HAD GOTTEN a little sleep from the battle, and in my case, a lot of sleep, healing is hard work. When I wake from my nap, I am still limping slightly, but it is so much better. I get some food and go right back to sleep.

The next morning, I am summoned to the conference room for a Summit meeting with the area leaders here. This time, it is just the leaders, no delegates or any betas, much to Jameson's dismay. Just the six of us and the recorder.

I am now placed at the head of the table with the others spread around the large table. There is one empty seat where the Western leader should be sitting. We all look at that seat and feel her loss all over again. The recorder is sitting behind us with her equipment, just waiting to do her job.

"All right. I call to order this emergency Summit meeting. "My grandfather tells the recorder.

My turn. "The funeral pyre for our lost shifters will be held as per tradition at midnight. I would appreciate it if everyone stayed long enough to honor our dead." Everyone agreed. "I know we lost a lot of people, but I would like to go around and have the area leaders of each region list the dead from your area. These brave shifters just lost their lives for the sake of our kind; they should be honored." I point to Franklin to start since he is on my right.

He clears his throat and lists the twenty names of the people he lost.

Carlos is next to him, and he does the same. He lists every one of the twelve souls that he lost in the battle.

Elena is next. "The council was unable to attend, other than myself, which they regret. But as the council member, I will read off the names for the Western region, starting with Sarah McClain, Western Region leader." She then lists the names of the remaining twelve others that were lost from the Western area.

My grandfather starts for the Central Region, listing five names, then my grandmother lists the remaining five names to be recorded.

"May you be reborn with pride," we all say at once. We all take a moment of silence before moving on.

"Did anyone get a number of the witches that were killed?" I ask.

Carlos nodded. "Yes, there were two hundred and seventeen." He pauses to look at the paper in front of him. "Six were injured, treated, and locked up for questioning. One group of twenty fled the scene, but not the main three we were watching for; they are all dead."

"A lot of lost lives for nothing," Elena whispers. I don't think anyone was meant to hear.

"One more thing," I go on. "We need to replace Sarah and give the Western territory a new leader. It has to be done, and soon." That area needs a leader appointed by us, or there will be a power vacuum drawing in all the shifters we don't want. "I nominate Anna."

Everyone looks at me. "Hear me out, Anna is not new to power. And she may be young in this life, but she has led areas before."

"I hate to be the one to go against you, dear," Carlos speaks up. "Because you have a lot of respect in my book. But that girl is a tiny little slip of a girl and an even smaller dog. She will be eaten alive."

"I hate to agree, but he is correct," Franklin adds.

"She is stronger than she looks. Size doesn't mean everything," I state. "Do you know that she took a fireball to the chest yesterday? And she ate the fire and walked away?" They did not know this, if I could judge by the looks I am now receiving. "I am not saying I want to lose my friend, but I truly think she will excel at the job."

"Well..." Elena starts drawing everyone's attention. "...Maybe we could put her there as an Interim. And if things work out at the next Summit meeting, which is scheduled to be in the west anyway, we can appoint her as the leader." She looks at everyone, then turns back to me. "But if it doesn't work, then we replace her. Do you agree?"

Reluctantly, I nod. "Let's put it to a vote. All those in favor of an interim leader. Being Anna. Say aye."

My grandparents, Elena, and I are for yes.

"Those against it." Not surprisingly, Franklin and Carlos say no.

"Since there is only one vote for the Central Region," Elena says, but stops me when I am about to interrupt. "That's three votes against two, making Anna our new area leader, temporarily. If she accepts."

Granny picks up the phone and presses a button. "Can you please send Anna in here?" She hangs up the phone.

Anna

There is a knock on my bedroom door as I am coming out of the bathroom. "Coming." If they had shown up five minutes ago, I would have been naked as a jaybird. I heard Cadence say that once, and now it's mine. I slip my feet into my shoes as I head for the door. I open it to see Emily, the beta female.

"You are being summoned to the conference room," she tells me, then turns around to lead me down the hall even though I know where I am going.

I am not sure what I did to warrant being called to the conference room when I know for a fact that they are having a Summit meeting in there. Before I can think too much about it, or what I could have possibly done, Emily is hitting the button for the intercom, kind of like a doorbell. "Send her in," comes from the little speaker.

Emily steps back and allows me to move past her into the room. She closes the door behind me, startling me, and my heart jumps into my throat.

Cadence laughs, which breaks the tension that I had been tightening in my body, making me unable to move. She knows how uncomfortable I get at times like this.

"Please come over here, Anna," the woman called Elena says. I believe she is part of the shifter council, but I'm not sure. I do as she says and make my way over to the table, then sit in the empty chair when she indicates it.

What the hell is going on here? Why am I even here when these meetings are always super secretive? The people involved cannot even speak about what happens in here when they leave those doors.

It's almost like that paper that Rose had me sign right after Cadence got here. Something about not running my mouth off. Where it doesn't belong. Now I know what a non-disclosure agreement is. I am not dumb, but it sounds better that way. I wonder if Cady even knows I signed that paper.

"Anna..." Elena says, bringing me out of that hamster wheel I call my brain. Unfortunately, I don't think it's the first time she has said my name. If her tone is anything to go by.

"I'm sorry, what?" I lock gazes with her.

She chuckles quietly. "Now that I have your attention, don't make me second-guess my vote. We have placed a vote, and you were voted in as the new Western leader, if you want to, of course. It could be a trial of three months, but Cadence speaks highly of you."

An area leader? They want me to pack up and move to California? I look to Cady, and she smiles and nods.

Do I want to be the Western leader? All very good questions. "How long do I have to decide?" I counter. This is a big, changing decision, not one that should be made on a whim. I need to go over it all. I must think this through properly. Without these people staring at me expectantly.

Elena looked around the table at the other leaders. I think she thought I would jump right into this without even thinking it over.

I am pretty sure the Northern and Southern leaders thought exactly that, by the way they are looking at me now. I think by asking that question, I might have gained a little bit of respect from the two of them.

"We would need to know before the funeral tonight, if possible. First thing in the morning, all the area leaders will be headed back to their own territory, and if you decide to lead the West, that's when you will need to be ready to leave with the betas."

I nod. "I can let you know by then."

"Good. You are dismissed." Alrighty then.

I thank them and make my exit. On autopilot now, I make my way to the front door. That is the closest exit. I need air now. I need space. I need to have my feet pounding the earth. Since I cannot be in animal form, that means human feet.

As soon as I step out the door, my feet are already moving, carrying me away from the house at a fast pace. I have always loved running. Running is my outlet for everything in life. Including thinking through tough decisions.

I returned to the house in time to have lunch with my friends. I am bound and determined to have a normal day. Cadence does not say anything about the decision weighing over my head. We both pretend it is not there, like a big elephant in the middle of a room, or a courtyard in this case.

By supper time, I have made up my mind. I haven't told anyone my decision yet, though.

When the clock hits eleven, I make my way down to the west fence, where just yesterday there was a giant hole. Now the hole has been boarded up. Just cheap plywood, but it is covered.

There is a massive funeral pyre, as per tradition. For centuries, we have burned our dead, sending them back to the Goddess's loving arms so she can return them to us.

I spot Cadence and the other area leaders on the other side of the pyre. I make my way over to them. As I approach, they'll turn their attention to me expectantly.

"I guess I am going to be a Cali girl for at least the next three months," I tell them excitedly.

After spending the day thinking about this, I believe it is the right decision for my own future. I need to get out and make my own life and not spend my life under the wing, or flaming paw in this case, of my best friend.

Cadence squeals and wraps me in a hug. Drawing the attention of... Well, everyone. The area leaders clapped me on the back or shook my hand.

Elena nods, then steps away. "Can I have everyone's attention, please. Can we settle down? We will begin in a moment, but I wanted to announce our new Western Region leader, Anna." She motions to me. I smile and square my shoulders. I want to make them all proud.

I think I catch a look of something from the betas... My betas, but when I look back, it is gone.

Elena starts the proceedings right on time. "We are gathered here to honor our fallen brothers and sisters. These shifters died honorably in a battle of life and death. As you see, there are five layers."

Franklin steps up to the side of her. "The bottom represents Earth. We have the twenty-two who died from the North. "We all look to the bottom layer, where you can see the bodies stacked repeatedly. "May your souls be grounded in the Goddess's grace."

"Next, we have the Central region, these ten shifters representing air for the east," Rose says this line. Then Robert joins her. "May your souls blow through this life straight into the Goddess's arms."

"For the Southern Region, we have twelve souls representing fire. May your passion always bring you back into the Goddess's arms." Carlos adds.

I step up then. "We have the twelve fallen soldiers from the west. May your souls flow straight into the Goddess's arms." I step back into line with the other leaders.

Elena steps up again. "You will see that the Western leader is on top. Representing Spirit. May our fallen leader lead you all back to the goddess safely."

Right as she is about to signal the men with the torches, I squeak and grab my stomach. Suddenly, out of nowhere, it feels as if a blowtorch has gone off in my stomach. I cry out once more, drawing the attention of the entire crowd. Everyone is watching me as I double over in pain. What the hell is happening?

I dropped to the ground as the blowtorch moved to engulf my entire body. Did the fire I got hit with in the battle have a delayed effect? Am I now dying? Or is my animal coming back to me?

In a way, that is exactly what it feels like, but this is so much worse than the first time. What could that potion or the fire do to me that could cause so much pain that I am completely unaware of what is going on around me?

That's when the tingle of the change starts. How can I feel that all over the flames are eating me alive? I have no freaking clue.

Now is when my body will start to shrink, compress in on itself, and turn into a little ankle biter everybody hates. Only that doesn't happen.

Instead of my body compressing, it starts to... Stretch? My mass feels as if it is growing larger, giving the fire more surface area to burn me alive with.

After a while, I am not sure how long because time is hard to determine when you are being burned alive, the fire starts to recede.

Sounds start to trickle back to me, and I hear gasps of disbelief. Someone, I am not sure who, says, "That's not possible."

I opened my eyes to try to see what's not possible and what everyone is talking about, and see... tree branches. How did I get up here? When I looked down, trying to figure out how to get out of the tree, I found out I was not in the tree. I am as big as the tree.

I can see the very top of the pyre below me that holds the bodies of our fallen shifters. That thing was over nine feet tall, and I am still a way from that. I squeak and go to step back, but the squeak comes out as sparks of fire, and they shoot straight at Sarah's body.

Because the pyre was filled with so many flammable materials, one little spark from me lit it up like the Fourth of July.

I try again to back up but end up with my rear end hitting the boards covering the hole in the fence. My very long tail just pushed the boards out of the way like they weren't even there.

The fire is still right in my face, and I can't go any further back, but the shiny red scales that are now covering every inch of my body are somehow protecting me from the flames.

"Well, that was a surprise," Cadence states the obvious.

The End... For now!

CHAPTER THIRTY-FOUR

Epilogue

THE SOUND OF A knock on the door to my hotel suite reverberates through the room. As Madi is attempting to place the veil into my hair. She has been cussing for the last 5 minutes trying to figure out how the attached clip will fit into my hair.

I start to turn, but Madi stops me with a firm hand on the side of my head. "No ma'am. I just got this figured out. If you move now, I will have to start all over again. Come in." the last, she says in response to the knock.

The door opens to reveal my father is decked out in his finest suit. "Are you read…?" He starts but cuts himself off as he comes all the way into the room and gets a good look at me. I bring my gaze to the mirror in front of me to see what he is seeing.

My long blue-black hair is pulled up into some complicated updo that Madi is still trying to attach the clip to. The stylist and make-up artists just left. After leaving my hair into this gorgeous style, and my makeup perfect. The whole package leaves me breathtaking to even me.

I am wearing a sleeveless mermaid style black wedding dress. Yes, black, since this is not a traditional wedding but a mix between a wedding and a hand fasting., I decided my dress should be black. Hunter, however, is wearing white. A little role reversal. The story of this lifetime.

I cannot believe we are finally here though. So many lifetimes, so many deaths, so many battles just for the right to be able to marry my own fated mate.

Two months ago, we finally defeated Felicia for good. Giving us the freedom to actually live our own lives. At least without looking over our shoulder for every evil witch to come ruin our big day. No, this time we get the happily ever after.

"All done." Madi declares then steps back, giving a little bow, even though all she did was attach the clip into my hair.

"Absolutely beautiful Cady." Anna says.

"The most beautiful bride I have ever seen" Mack adds beside me. She is wiping tears from her eyes. Already. If its this bad she will never make it to the ceremony.

All three hug me carefully. They are trying their best not to ruin the perfection of what everyone has worked so hard to achieve.

I turned toward my dad, and he walked right into my arms. "Yes, dad. I am ready. I have been ready for hundreds of years."

The ceremony we chose today is a good blend of a traditional wedding and a traditional Hand-fasting. This way we get to pick and choose what we want to keep and what we don't. Especially that little line that asks if anyone objects. If anyone objects, I will stick my hellcat on them. We will not be giving them a chance. We have waited long enough.

The girls line up in front of me, Madi, then Anna and then Mack. My dad and I line up behind them. "My little girl is all grown up and I am so very proud of the woman you have become, Cadence." He kisses me on the cheek. "Always remember that."

It would be just like my dad to make me cry just as the wedding march starts, but who cares? I take my place with the tears in my eyes and make my way down the aisle. Toward my future. There is no way I am wiping all of that carefully done makeup off. People will just have to deal with my tears.

We make our way down the aisle to where my mate waits for me. Elena is standing behind him, but I only have eyes for Hunter. As I stare into his beautiful blue eyes, all I can see is our happy future.

The vows are said, our hands are tied together, and then the moment I have been waiting several lifetimes for.

"You are now husband and wife. Hunter, kiss your bride already." A big smile lights up his face as he wraps his arms around me and then his lips touch mine. He kisses me as if we are alone. As it should be.

We are finally married. We made it. There is no stopping us now. We will live the life we should have been able to have so many times over.

We turned to face all our friends and family. Elena speaks from behind us. "Now, for the first time in hundreds of years, I would like to introduce you to Mr., Missus and Mini Riggs."

There is a split second of silence, then the room erupts into chaos. Cheers. As they figure out what the announcement meant.

---

4 Months Later- Cadence

The first thing I notice when I wake is the sound of his breathing. Slow, deep, and steady, the way it always is when Hunter sleeps with his arm hooked over my side, holding on to his child, his body pressed along the length of mine. It's a sound that means home, no matter what city, lifetime, or body we've found ourselves in. And it still makes my chest ache in the best way.

The second thing I notice is the sunlight pooling across the sheets, turning them gold. We never meant to fall asleep like this, tangled in each other long after midnight, but neither of us was willing to break the spell last night had cast over us.

I tilt my head, brushing my cheek against the inside of his arm. "Morning," I murmur. My voice is rough with sleep, and it pulls one of his eyes open. That blue, it's a color I've known through centuries, through blood and war and quiet stolen moments, and it still manages to knock the breath out of me.

"You were supposed to wake me before sunrise," he says, his voice warm and teasing, like he knows damn well I had no intention of doing any such thing.

"I tried," I say, though the half-smile tugging at my mouth betrays me. "You growl when you're sleeping. It's intimidating."

He huffs out a laugh and props himself on one elbow, his hand sliding from my waist to my hip and over the swell of my belly before returning to my hip. His thumb traces idle circles through the thin fabric of the oversized shirt I'm wearing—his shirt. The one he'd pulled off last night just before.

My breath catches. The memory of his mouth against my skin, the heat of him, the way his name broke from me like a prayer, it's all still vivid enough that my body remembers every detail. I can see in the sharp curve of his smile that he remembers, too.

"Cadence..." he says my name like it's the only word that's ever mattered, and then he's leaning down to kiss me. Slow at first, a gentle brush of lips, before the hunger we never really tame sparks between us again. My fingers curl into the back of his neck, and the kiss deepens until there's no air left between us.

The world outside this bed doesn't exist for a while. There's only the slide of his hand under my shirt, the way his palm molds to my side, the low rumble in his chest when I press closer. I let my leg hook over his hip, drawing him in until I can feel the heat of him through the thin barrier of his boxers. This is not an easy task anymore. He makes a sound half groan, half growl that goes straight to my core.

We've had lifetimes of stolen nights like this, but the difference now is we're free. No curses hanging over our heads. No enemies waiting to rip us apart the moment we let our guard down. Just him. Just me. And the way we've always fit together like nothing in the world could break us.

His hand slides higher, fingers brushing over my breast, and my breath stutters. "Hunter..." I whisper, my voice trembling with need.

"Tell me to stop," he says, though we both know I won't. I never do.

Instead, I tug at his waistband, and that's all the encouragement he needs. The rest of his clothes are gone in moments, mine following until nothing separates us. His mouth finds my neck, tracing the line of my pulse before claiming my lips again.

When he enters me, it's slow—so achingly slow—that I dig my nails into his back. We move together in a rhythm we've always known, one that feels older than either of us, older than this lifetime. Each thrust is a promise, each kiss a reminder that no matter how many times we've lost each other, we've always found our way back.

I cling to him, burying my face against his shoulder, breathing in the scent that's always been his warm cedar and something wilder, something that doesn't belong to this world. My body arches, every nerve lit up, and when release crashes through me, it's with his name on my lips. He follows me over the edge seconds later, holding me as though letting go isn't an option.

For a long time afterward, we just lie there, our breathing slowly syncing again. My head rests against his chest, listening to that steady heartbeat I've chased across centuries. His fingers comb lazily through my hair.

"Do you ever think about it?" I ask quietly.

"About what?"

"All the lifetimes we could've had if she hadn't found us. If she hadn't..." I can't even say Felicia's name without feeling the old ache flare.

Hunter's hand stills in my hair. "I used to. A lot. But that's not our story anymore. We've got this life now, and I'm not wasting a second of it looking back."

I nod, but the unease in my chest doesn't completely fade. We might have defeated her six months ago, but the shadows she left behind are still there—lurking, waiting. And I can't shake the feeling that peace for us is a fragile thing.

He must see it on my face because he tips my chin up, meeting my gaze. "We've survived everything. And we'll survive whatever's next. Together."

It's the "together" that steadies me. That's the part I can believe in without hesitation.

Eventually, we drag ourselves out of bed, though neither of us makes much effort to hurry. The rest of the world can wait a little longer. There's coffee to be made, a baby shower to prepare for, and the easy kind of silence that only comes from centuries of knowing someone's every breath.

But when I catch my reflection in the window, my chest tightens. For a heartbeat, it isn't my own face looking back, it's the echo of another lifetime, another version of me, standing beside a blood-soaked altar. Hunter's voice pulls me back, grounding me in the here and now, but the image lingers like a warning.

Some part of me knows this calm won't last forever. That whatever comes next will test us again.

I only hope, when it does, we'll still be standing. The three of us.

Afterword

I hope you have enjoyed Cadence and Hunter's story. If you enjoyed the world, please be on the lookout for upcoming books. Including Anna's story as she takes California by storm. What is in store for Madison? We will have to wait and see where this world takes her.

Coming Soon

Acknowledgements

I want to first thank every person that helped me throughout this process. From my family that let me talk endlessly to my beta readers to the editors and formatters and cover designer. Especially the author who helped with almost every step, from information to formatting. You know how you are and a big thank you to you. Thank you all for everything. This could not have been possible without you.

Misty Kemp has a passion for writing romance, with a twist of fantasy. Her debut novel Black Dawn is a shape-shifter romance novel. The first in a series. When she is not writing her own epic love stories, she enjoys filling her time reading. She reads every chance she gets. She hopes her readers will enjoy her captivating setting and intriguing characters.

www.ingramcontent.com/pod-product-compliance
Lightning Source LLC
Chambersburg PA
CBHW071116100726
47908CB00008B/2388